SECRET PRINCE'S CHRISTMAS SEDUCTION

SECRET PRINCE'S CHRISTMAS SEDUCTION

CAROL MARINELLI

MILLS & BOON

First published in Great Britain 2019
by Mills & Boon, an imprint of HarperCollins*Publishers*
1 London Bridge Street, London, SE1 9GF

Large Print edition 2020

ISBN: 978-0-263-08436-8

MIX
Paper from
responsible sources
FSC® C007454

This book is produced from independently certified FSC™ paper to ensure responsible forest management. For more information visit www.harpercollins.co.uk/green.

Printed and bound in Great Britain
by CPI Group (UK) Ltd, Croydon, CR0 4YY

PROLOGUE

'THANKS, BUT I'M really hoping to be spending Christmas with my family.' Realising that she might have come across as ungrateful, Antonietta immediately apologised. 'It's very kind of you to invite me, but…'

'I get it.' Aurora shrugged as she carried on helping Antonietta to unpack. 'You didn't come to Silibri to spend Christmas Day with the Messinas.'

'Ah, but you're a Caruso now!' Antonietta smiled.

The cemetery in the village of Silibri, where Antonietta had loved to wander, held many names, but there were a few constants, and Caruso, Messina and Ricci were the prominent ones.

Especially Ricci.

The Ricci family extended across the southwest region of Sicily and beyond, but Silibri was its epicentre. Antonietta's father, who was the chief fire officer and a prominent landowner, was well connected and held in high regard.

'Do you know...?' Antonietta paused in hanging up the few clothes she owned. 'If I *had* married Sylvester then I wouldn't even have had to change my surname. I would still be Antonietta Ricci.'

'Yes, and you would be married to your second cousin and living in a property on the grounds of your father's home, with Sylvester working for him.'

'True...' Antonietta started to say, but then faltered.

She had run away on her wedding day, five years ago, in rather spectacular style—climbing out of the bedroom window as her father waited outside to take her to the packed church. Sylvester was popular in the village, and a member of her extended family, so the fallout had been dire—her family had rejected her completely. Letters and emails had gone unanswered and her mother hung up on her whenever she called to try and make her case.

She had spent four years living and working in France, but though she had persisted with the language, and made friends there, it had never felt like home. So she had come back to Silibri, for Aurora and Nico's wedding, but there had been no welcome committee to greet her. Instead she had been shunned by both her immediate and extended family.

Rejecting Sylvester, and so publicly, had been taken as a rejection of them and their closed family values and traditions.

Since Nico and Aurora's wedding she had been working at Nico's grand hotel in Rome, as a chambermaid. But Rome was not home either, and she had often confided to her friend how she missed Silibri.

Antonietta had wanted one final chance to make amends, and Aurora had offered a solution—she could work as a chambermaid in Nico's new hotel in Silibri while training part-time as a massage therapist. The old monastery there had been painstakingly rebuilt, and refurbished to Nico's exacting standards, and it was more a luxurious retreat than a hotel. To train there would be a career boost indeed.

It was an opportunity that Antonietta didn't want to miss—but, given the level of animosity towards her, it was clear she would struggle to live in the village. Aurora had had a solution to that too—there was a small stone cottage, set on the cliff-edge, and Aurora had said she was more than welcome to use it.

'The internet connection is terrible there and it's too close to the helipad and hangar for the guests,' Aurora had explained, 'so it's just sitting empty.'

'Hopefully I shan't need it for too long,' Antonietta had replied. 'Once my family know that I'm back and working…'

She had seen the doubtful look flicker in her dear friend's eyes. The same doubtful look that flickered now, as Antonietta insisted she would be back with her family for the festivities.

'Antonietta…?'

She heard the question in her friend's voice and braced herself. Aurora was as outspoken as Antonietta was quiet, but till now her friend had refrained from stating the obvious.

'It's been five years since your family have spoken to you…'

'I know that,' Antonietta said. 'But it's not as if I've actually given them much opportunity to do so.'

'You came back for my wedding,' Aurora pointed out. 'And you were ignored by them.'

'I think they were just shocked to see me. But once they know I'm properly here, that I'm back for good…'

Aurora sat down on the bed but Antonietta remained standing, not wanting to have the conversation that was to come.

'It's been *years*,' Aurora said again. 'You were only twenty-one when it happened, and now you are close to turning twenty-six! Isn't it time to stop beating yourself up?'

'But I'm not,' Antonietta said. 'It's been an amazing five years. I've travelled and I've learnt a new language. It's not as if I'm walking around in sackcloth and ashes—most of the time life is wonderful. It's just at…'

Just at other times.

Times that should surely be spent with family.

'Christmas is especially hard,' Antonietta admitted. 'It is then that I miss them the most.

And I find it hard to believe that they don't think of me and miss me also. Especially my mother. I want to give them one final chance…'

'Fair enough—but what about fun?' Aurora persisted. 'I get that it hasn't been all doom and gloom, but you haven't spoken of any friends. I never hear you saying you're going on a date…'

'*You* never dated anyone until Nico,' Antonietta said rather defensively.

'Only because I have loved Nico my entire life,' Aurora said. 'No one compared. But at least I tried once…'

They both laughed as they recalled Aurora's attempt to get over Nico by getting off with a fireman, but then Antonietta's laughter died away. There was a very good reason she hadn't dated. One that she hadn't even shared with her closest friend. It wasn't just the fact that Sylvester was her second cousin that had caused Antonietta to flee on her wedding day. It had been her dread of their wedding night.

Sylvester's kisses had repulsed Antonietta, and the rough, urgent roaming of his hands had terrified her. And her reluctance to partake had infuriated *him*.

It had all come to a head for Antonietta in the weeks before the planned wedding, when she had come to dread time spent alone with her fiancé. On more than a couple of occasions he had almost overpowered her, and Antonietta had been forced to plead with Sylvester and say that she was saving herself for her wedding night.

'Frigida,' he had called her angrily.

And very possibly she was, Antonietta had concluded, because to this day the thought of being intimate with a man left her cold.

At the time she had tried voicing her fears about it to her *mamma*, but her advice had been less than reassuring. Her *mamma* had told her that once she was married it was her wifely duty to perform *'once a week to keep him happy'*.

As the wedding night had loomed closer, so had Antonietta's sense of dread. And that feeling of dread, whenever she thought of kissing a man, let alone being intimate with a man, had stayed with her.

She wished she could speak about it with Aurora. But her friend was so confident with her sexuality, and so deliriously happy in her marriage that instead of confiding in her, Antonietta remained eternally private and kept the darkest part of her soul to herself.

'It's time to live a little,' Aurora pushed now.

'I agree.' Antonietta nodded, even if she didn't quite believe it herself. 'But first I have to give my parents this chance to forgive me.'

'For *what*, Antonietta?' Aurora was blunt. 'Sylvester was your second cousin; the fact is they just wanted to keep their money in the family and keep the Ricci name strong—'

'Even so…' It was Antonietta who interrupted now. 'I shamed my parents in front of their entire family. I left Sylvester standing at the altar! You saw the fallout, Aurora…'

'Yes…'

Apparently a huge fight had broken out in the church. Antonietta hadn't hung around to witness it, though; she had timed it so she had been on the train out of Silibri by then.

'I miss having a family.' It was the simple truth. 'They are not perfect—I know that—but I miss having them in my life. And even if we cannot reconcile I feel there is unfinished business between us. Even if it is a final goodbye then I want it to be said face to face.'

'Well, the offer's there if you change your mind,' Aurora said. 'Nico and I want Gabe to celebrate his first Christmas in Silibri…' Her voice trailed off as she pulled a swathe of scarlet fabric from Antonietta's case. 'This is beautiful—where did you get it?'

'Paris.' Antonietta smiled and ran her hands fondly over the fabric. 'I bought it just after I arrived there.' It had been a late summer's day and, having just written to her parents, she had been buoyed by the prospect of reconciliation. 'I was walking through Place Saint-Pierre and I wandered into a fabric store.'

She had decided to celebrate her happy mood and there amongst the brocades and velvets she had found a bolt of stunning crimson silk and bought a length.

'You have had it all this time and done nothing with it?' Aurora checked as Antonietta wrapped it back in its tissue paper and placed it in the bottom drawer of a heavy wooden chest. 'You *cannot* leave this hiding in a drawer.'

'I might make some cushions with it.'

'Cushions?' Aurora was aghast. 'That fabric deserves to be made into a dress and taken out!'

'Oh? And when will I ever wear it?'

'As a last resort you can wear it in your coffin,' Aurora said with typical Sicilian dark humour. 'You can lie there dead and people can say *Look how beautiful she almost was!* Give it to me and let me make something with it.'

Aurora was a brilliant seamstress, and would certainly make something beautiful, but it was almost reluctantly that Antonietta handed over the fabric.

'Let me get your measurements,' Aurora said.

'I don't have a tape measure.'

But of course Aurora did. And so, instead of unpacking, Antonietta stood, feeling awkward and shy in her underwear, holding her long, straight black hair up as Aurora took her measurements down to the last detail.

'You are *so* slim,' Aurora said as she wrote them all down. 'One of my legs is the size of your waist.'

'Rubbish!'

They were lifelong best friends and complete opposites. Aurora was all rippling curls and curves, and she exuded confidence, whereas Antonietta was as reserved and as slender as her shadow that now fell on the stone wall. The evening was cool, rather than cold, but the year was certainly moving into winter, and she shivered as Aurora took her time, writing down the measurements.

Antonietta tried to hurry her along. 'Nico will be here for you soon,' she warned.

He was checking on the hotel while Aurora helped her settle in, but soon his helicopter would come to return both him and Aurora to their residence in Rome.

'Aren't you going to drop in and visit your parents before you head back?'

'I am avoiding them.' Aurora rolled her eyes. 'Can you believe they want Nico to employ my lazy, good-for-nothing brother as chief groundskeeper for the Old Monastery?'

Antonietta laughed. Aurora's brother was lazy indeed.

'It's no joke,' Aurora said. 'You would need a scythe to get to work if Nico relented. My brother is as bone idle as yours, but of course now me and Nico are married he seems to think that Nico owes him a job!'

'I hope Nico didn't feel obliged to employ *me...*'

'Don't be ridiculous.' Aurora cut her off. 'You are a hard worker and the Old Monastery is lucky to have you.'

Even so, it was a huge favour for them to give her this cottage as she worked on making amends for the past.

The sound of Nico's chopper starting up made Aurora look out of the window. 'There he is...' She kissed her friend on both cheeks and gave her a hug. 'Good luck starting work and I'll see you on Christmas Eve—if not before. And I mean it, Antonietta. If things don't work out with your family, the offer to join us is there.'

'Thank you,' Antonietta said. 'But Christmas is still a couple of months away; there is plenty of time for things to sort themselves out.'

'You'll be okay?' Aurora checked. 'You really are a bit cut off here.'

'I'll be fine,' Antonietta assured her. 'Thanks so much for this.'

Nico did not come into the cottage; instead

he headed straight to the chopper and Antonietta watched as Aurora joined him. They were clearly both happy to be heading back to Rome and little Gabe, who would soon be turning one. She was glad that Nico hadn't dropped in. She was starting work soon, and didn't want her co-workers thinking that she had a direct line to the boss through her friend.

It felt odd, though, after Aurora had gone and she was truly alone.

The cottage was beautifully furnished, with a modern kitchen and a cosy living area, and she wandered through it, taking in not just the furnishings but the stunning view of the ocean from her bedroom. No beach was visible, just choppy waves and crashing foam. Despite the cool evening she opened the window, just to drown out the crippling silence that had descended since Aurora had left.

She was home, Antonietta told herself.

Not that it felt like it.

In truth, Silibri never had.

Antonietta had never quite felt she belonged.

CHAPTER ONE

Six weeks later

ANTONIETTA WAS UP long before the Sicilian winter sun. For a while she lay in the dark bedroom of her little stone cottage, listening to the sound of the waves rolling in and crashing on the rocks below. It might have worked in the meditation of monks of old, and it might be a tranquil backdrop for the guests, but it brought little peace to Antonietta.

It was two weeks until Christmas and since her return there had been little progress with her family. If anything the situation had worsened, with rude stares and muttered insults whenever she ventured into the village, and when she had gone to her parents' home the door had been closed in her face by her father.

Yet she had glimpsed a pained look in her

mother's eyes from the hallway—as if her *mamma* had something she wanted to say.

It was for that reason Antonietta persisted.

Sylvester had married and moved away from the village, so there was little chance of bumping into him. And it was good to walk on the beach or in the hillsides she knew. Work was going incredibly well too; her colleagues were friendly and supportive and her training was first class.

Having showered, she went into her wardrobe to select her uniform. It varied—when she was working at the Oratory she wore white, but today she was working on cleaning the suites, so would need her regular uniform.

But as she went to take out her uniform her fingers lingered on the new addition to her wardrobe.

Yes, Aurora was a wonderful seamstress indeed, and the scarlet dress had arrived yesterday! However, just as Antonietta had been reluctant to hand over the fabric, she was even more reluctant to try it on. The dress was bold and sensual and everything she was not.

Still, there was not time for lingering. Her

shift started soon, so she pulled out her uniform and got dressed.

The uniforms were actually stunning: the Persian orange linen went well with her olive skin and her slender figure suited the cut of the dress. Antonietta wore no make-up, either in or out of work, so getting ready didn't take long. She pulled her hair into a neat ponytail and then, having slipped on a jacket, made her way across the grounds towards the monastery.

Her little cottage was quite some distance from the main building. Still, it was a pleasant walk, with the sky turning to navy as the sleepy stars readied themselves to fade for the day, and there was a crisp, salt-laden breeze coming in from the Mediterranean.

And there was already activity at the Old Monastery!

A couple of dark-suited gentlemen were walking around the perimeter of the building and Pino, the chief concierge, was looking *very* dapper this morning as he greeted her warmly. '*Buongiorno*, Antonietta.'

'*Buongiorno*, Pino,' she responded.

'We have a new guest!'

The hotel housed many guests, but with the extra security visible Antonietta had already guessed there was a VIP in residence.

Pino loved to gossip and was determined to fill her in. 'We are to address him as Signor Louis Dupont. However…' Pino tapped the side of his nose '…the truth is he is really—'

'Pino…' Antonietta interrupted.

She adored Pino, and always arrived early to allow herself time to chat with him. Pino had recently lost his beloved wife of forty years, Rosa, and she knew that work was the only thing keeping him sane. Still, given that Antonietta was already a main source of gossip in the village, she refused to partake in it now.

'If that is how he wants to be addressed, then that is enough for me.'

'Fair enough,' Pino said, and then he took a proper look at her. 'How are you doing, Antonietta?'

'I'm getting there,' she said, touched that with all that was going on in his world he still took the time to ask about her. 'How about you?'

'I'm not looking forward to Christmas. Rosa

always made it so special. It was her favourite time of the year.'

'What will you do? Are you going to visit your daughter?'

'No, it is her husband's family's turn this year, so I've told Francesca that I'll work. I decided that would be better than sitting at home alone. What about you—has there been any progress with your family?'

'None,' Antonietta admitted. 'I have been to the house several times but they still refuse to speak with me, and my trips to the village are less than pleasant. Perhaps it's time I accept that I'm not wanted here.'

'Not true,' Pino said. 'Not everyone is a Ricci—or related to one.'

'It feels like it.'

'Things will get better.'

'Perhaps—if I live to be a hundred!'

They shared a small wry smile. Both knew only too well that grudges lasted for a very long time in Silibri.

'You're doing well at work,' Pino pointed out.

'Yes!'

And the fact that she had committed to the

therapy course was the main reason Antonietta had stayed even when it had become clear that her family did not want her around. With each shift, both as a chambermaid and while training as a therapist, she fell in love with her work a little more. Working at the Old Monastery was so different from the bars and café jobs that had supported her while she lived in France, and she preferred the tranquil nature of Silibri to the hustle and bustle of Rome.

'Work has been my saviour,' she admitted.

'And mine,' Pino agreed.

As she walked into the softly lit foyer the gorgeous scent of pine reached her, and Antonietta took a moment to breathe it in. Apart from the stunning Nebrodi fir tree, adorned with citrus fruits, there were no other Christmas decorations. As Nico had pointed out, many of their guests were retreating to *escape* Christmas, and did not need constant reminders—but Aurora, being Aurora, had insisted on at least a tree.

Still, thought Antonietta, as magnificent and splendid as the tree was, it was just a token, and somehow it just didn't *feel* like Christmas once had in Silibri.

Heading into the staff room, she dropped off her bag and jacket and made her way to the morning briefing from Maria, the head of housekeeping.

Francesca, the regional manager, was also in early, and was looking on as the chambermaids were informed that a new guest had just arrived into the August Suite, which was *the* premier suite of the hotel.

'I don't have his photo yet,' said Maria.

All the staff would be shown his photograph, so he could be recognised and greeted appropriately at all times, and so that all charges could be added to his suite without any formalities.

'Signor Dupont is to be given top priority,' Francesca cut in. 'If there are any issues you are to report them directly to me.'

Ah, so *that* was the reason she was here so early, Antonietta thought. She was always very aware of Francesca. Antonietta liked her, but because Francesca was a close friend of her mother there was a certain guardedness between them.

'Antonietta, that is where you shall be working today,' Maria continued with the handover. 'When you are not busy, you can assist Chi-Chi in the other superior suites, but Signor Dupont is to take priority at all times.'

Antonietta had been surprised at how quickly she had moved through the ranks. She was now regularly allocated the most important guests and Francesca had told her she was perfect for the role.

The August, Starlight and Temple Suites were sumptuous indeed, and the guests they housed could be anything from visiting royalty to rock stars recovering from their excesses, or even movie stars recuperating after a little nip and tuck.

The reason that Antonietta was so perfectly suited to working in the suites was her rather private nature. She had enough problems of her own and didn't care to delve into other people's. Nor did she have stars in her eyes, and she was not dumbstruck by celebrity, fame or title. Generally polite conversation was all that was required, and Antonietta could certainly do that. Silence was merited on occasion, and she was more than happy to oblige. She was polite to the guests, if a little distant, but she did her work quietly and well and let the guests be.

At the end of the handover, Francesca pulled Antonietta aside and gave her the pager for the August Suite. She offered a little more information.

'Signor Dupont has declined the services of a butler. He has stated that he wants privacy and is not to be unnecessarily disturbed. Perhaps you can sort out with him the best time to service his suite—he might want to get it over and done with—but I shall leave that to you.'

A guest in the August Suite could have the rooms serviced a hundred times a day if he so demanded.

'Also, Signor Dupont might need some assistance getting out of bed. If he—'

'I am not a nurse,' Antonietta interrupted. She had firm boundaries.

'I know that,' Francesca said, and gave her rather surly chambermaid a tight smile. 'Signor Dupont already has a nurse—although he seems rather testy and insists that he does not need one. Should he require her assistance, she can be paged. I should warn you that he is very bruised, so don't be shocked.'

'Okay.'

'Antonietta, I probably shouldn't tell you who he is, but—'

'Then please don't,' Antonietta cut in.

For her it really was as simple as that. She did not gossip and she did not listen to gossip either. Oh, the staff here were wonderful, and their gossip was never malicious. Certainly it would not reach the press, which was why there were so many exclusive guests at the hotel.

The same courtesy was extended in the village. The locals were all thrilled at the vibrancy that had returned to the town with the new hotel, and so the Silibri people looked after its guests as their own. In fact, they looked after the guests *better* than their own—Antonietta had been treated shabbily by many of them.

'I don't want to know his real name, Francesca,' she said now, 'because then I might slip up and use it. Tell me only what I need to know.'

'Very well—he has his own security detail and you will need to show them your ID. He's booked in until Christmas Eve. Although, from what I gather, I believe it is doubtful he will last until then.'

'He's dying?' Antonietta frowned.

'No!' Francesca laughed. 'I meant he will grow bored. Now, he wants coffee to be delivered promptly at seven.'

'Then I had better get on.'

Francesca carried on chatting as they both made their way to the kitchen. 'I have just finalised the roster,' she told her. 'And I have you down for an early start on Christmas Day.'

Antonietta stopped in her tracks, and was about to open her mouth to protest, but then Francesca turned and she saw the resigned, almost sympathetic look on her manager's face. Francesca wasn't just telling her that she was to work on Christmas Day, Antonietta realised. Her mother must have made it clear to her friend that Antonietta would not be invited to partake in the family's festivities.

'Working is better than sitting alone in that cottage,' Francesca said as they resumed walking and headed into the kitchen. 'I shall be here too, and so will Pino and Chi-Chi…'

All the lonely hearts were working over Christmas then, Antonietta thought sadly.

'I'm on over Christmas too,' said Tony, the very portly head chef—which only confirmed Antonietta's thoughts.

Tony was married to his job, and put all his care and love into his food, and there was no exception this morning. There was a huge silver pot of coffee for their new guest, and cream and sugar, but there was also a basket of pastries and bread, a meat and cheese platter, and a fruit platter too. All the chefs, and especially Tony, could not refrain from adding Sicilian flair to every dish.

'Tony,' Antonietta pointed out as she checked the order, 'he only ordered coffee, but you have prepared a feast.'

'He is a *guest*.' Tony shrugged.

'And he's a big man!' Francesca said, holding out her hands high and wide. 'Huge! He needs to eat!'

It was the Silibri way—even in the poorest home there would be *biscotti* and *pizzelles* served alongside coffee. There was no point arguing, so Antonietta wheeled the trolley towards the elevator.

The monastery had been refurbished to perfection, and although it still looked ancient, it had all mod cons. Antonietta often saw the guests blink in surprise when they stepped behind a stone partition to reach the discreet elevator.

She took the elevator up to the top floor and, alone for a moment, slumped against the wall as she dwelt on the message behind Francesca's words. It really was time to accept that her family simply didn't want her. It was time to move on.

Where, though?

Back to France, perhaps? Or to Rome?

But she hadn't felt she had belonged in either place, and there was still her training to complete…

Catching sight of her reflection, she straightened up and gave herself a mental shake. It wasn't the guest's fault that she was feeling blue, and she put on her game face as she stepped out and wheeled the trolley across the cloister, past the Starlight and Temple Suites, and across to the August Suite.

A suited man stood as she neared. She had known guests to bring their own security detail before, but never to this extent. What with the extra guards outside and within, this guest must be important indeed.

The guard was not exactly friendly, but without a word he looked at the photo on her lanyard and then checked Antonietta's face before stepping aside to let her past.

She knocked gently on the large wooden door. There was no response so, as she'd been trained to do, Antonietta let herself in with a swipe of her key card. Once inside, she turned on a side light and wheeled the trolley through the dimly lit lounge and over to the entrance to the main bedroom. She gave the door a gentle knock.

No response.

Another gentle knock and then, as she carefully opened the door, Antonietta called his name. 'Signor Dupont?'

Again there was no response, and though the room was in darkness it was clear to her that he was asleep. His breathing was deep and even, and judging from his outline Antonietta could see that he lay on his stomach in the large four-poster bed, with a sheet covering him.

'I have coffee for you,' Antonietta said quietly. 'Would you like me to open the drapes? The sun is just about to rise.'

'Si.' He stirred in the bed as he gave his groggy reply.

Antonietta headed to the drapes to open them, though it was not a simple matter of pulling them apart. The windows were vast and the dark velvet curtains heavy; pulling with both hands on the cord was truly like parting the curtains at a theatre, as if a play was about to unfold before her eyes.

The August Suite was her favourite. It occupied an entire wing of the Old Monastery, which allowed for panoramic views. The view from the lounge looked across the ocean, and the dining room looked over the valley, but here in the master bedroom there was a view of the ancient temple ruins.

Antonietta drank it in for a moment. There, as fingers of red light spread across the sky, the ocean danced to the rising sun and she felt she could happily gaze on it for ever. The view, though, was not hers to enjoy just now.

Antonietta turned around, and as she did so she started slightly when she first laid eyes on the guest.

He was *nothing* like she had imagined. From Francesca's description she had been expecting a possibly aging, somewhat bedridden and rather large man. But, while he was indeed large, he was certainly not overweight. Instead he was incredibly tall, judging by the amount of space he took up in the large bed. He was also broad and muscular, and thankfully covered by the sheet where it mattered.

And she guessed he might be around thirty.

Francesca had been right, though, to warn her about the bruises, for they really were shocking—purple and black, they covered his arms and chest and one eye, and his top lip was swollen. Signor Dupont, or whatever his real name was, had thick black hair that was rather messy, and also very matted—Antonietta guessed with blood. Of course she made no comment, but for the first time she found herself more than a little curious as to what had happened to a guest.

'Poor decision,' Signor Dupont said, and she guessed he was referring to the sun, for he was shielding his eyes as he struggled to sit up in the bed.

'I can close them…' Antonietta offered.

'No, leave them.'

He would get used to the bright light soon, Rafe told himself, even as his pulse roared in his ears. But brighter than the sun were the shards of memory painfully surfacing in his brain—the absolute knowledge that this fall had been serious.

Rafe did not fear death for himself, but for a seemingly endless moment he had glimpsed the grief and chaos he would leave behind and had fought to right himself. He could not shake the memory of the looks of horror on his bodyguards' faces, the sense of panic all around, which seemed at odds with the soft voice speaking to him now.

'Would you like me to pour your coffee, Signor Dupont?'

For a moment he wondered who she was referring to. And then he remembered.

Ah, yes, security was extra-tight, for it would be disastrous if news of this near-miss leaked out.

So Rafe nodded and watched as the maid poured his drink, but as she removed one of the linen covers on the tray the sweet scent of bread and pastry reached him, and with it a wave of nausea.

'I only asked for coffee.'

'Ah, but you are in Silibri,' she responded. 'Here there is no such thing as "just coffee."'

'Please tell the chef that he is not to misinterpret my orders,' Rafe snapped.

'I shall pass that on.'

'Leave and take the trolley with you.' He dismissed her with a wave of his hand.

'Of course.'

Antonietta was only too happy to go. 'Testy' didn't come close to describing him. However, there was one thing that needed to be sorted out before she left. 'When would you like me to return and service the suite, Signor Du—?'

'Please!' His interruption was irritated rather

than polite, and his dark eyes held hers in reprimand. 'Don't call me that again. Just use my first name.'

'Very well.' Antonietta felt a nervous flutter in her stomach, and it had nothing to do with his surly tone, and more to do with the deep navy of his eyes, which reminded her of the sky that morning. 'So, Louis, when would you—?'

'Rafe!' he snapped, and then softened his tone. It was not her fault there were so many restrictions on publicising his identity. 'You are to call me Rafe. And, no, I do not want my room serviced. If you could make up the bed while I have my coffee, that will suffice.'

He moved to climb out of bed, but then perhaps he got dizzy, because instead of heading to the bedside chair he remained sitting on the edge with his head in his hands, his skin turning from pale to grey.

He should be in hospital, Antonietta thought. 'Would you like me to—?'

'I can manage,' he snapped.

They'd both spoken at the same time, and Antonietta had not finished her sentence. Now she did. 'Would you like me to fetch the nurse to help you get out of bed?'

For some reason what she said caused him to lift his head from his hands and look at her. Antonietta was sure he *almost* smiled, but then his expression changed to austere.

'I *don't* need a nurse and I *don't* need the bed linen changed. Please, just leave.'

His tone was still brusque, but Antonietta took no offence. It was clear to her that Louis—or rather Rafe—loathed being seen in a weakened state. He was holding tightly on to the bedside table with one hand, while the other gripped the mattress, and she was certain he would prefer to be alone than have anyone witness him like this.

'Would you like me to come back later?'

'No.' He gave a shake of his head, which must have hurt, because he halted midway. 'I really don't want to be disturbed today—if you could let everybody know?'

'I shall.'

'And could you block out the sun before you leave?'

It was a slightly oddly worded request, and

only then did she realise that Italian wasn't his first language. It took a second to place, but she soon realised that his Italian was tinged with an accent she loved—French.

She wanted to delve. For the first time ever Antonietta wanted to know more about a guest. He had asked that she use his real name—Rafe—and now she wanted to know it in full. She wanted to know where he was from and what had led him to this Silibri retreat to heal in secret.

Antonietta wanted to know *more* about this man.

But instead she wheeled out the trolley while the room was still light, and then returned. 'I'll close the drapes and then get out of your way. But, please, if you need anything then don't hesitate to page me.'

Rafe nodded and glanced at her, and was slightly bemused when he noticed her eyes. It wasn't so much that they were as black as treacle, and thickly lashed, it was more that he had never seen such sadness. Oh, it was not anything tangible—she was not downcast or grim—but there was an abject melancholy in them that tugged him out of deep introspection. And that was no mean feat, for Rafe had a lot on his mind.

An awful lot.

The black-eyed maid took out the trolley, and by the time she returned Rafe was back in bed. Before closing the drapes, she topped up the water by his bed.

'Thank you,' Rafe said, once the room was mercifully back to darkness. He actually meant it, for she had worked unobtrusively and had not, unlike so many others, pushed for conversation, nor dashed to help unasked. He almost smiled again when he remembered her offer to fetch the nurse rather than assist herself.

'What is your name?' he asked.

'Antonietta.'

And that was that.

Well, almost.

She wheeled the trolley back to the elevator and then went down to the kitchen and picked up the tablet to make a note of his requests. The internal computer system for the domestic staff was easy to navigate—she checked the box to say that he had declined having his suite serviced and added a note that he was not to be disturbed.

Yet she lingered a second.

His photo was up now, and she flushed as she looked at his elegant features. He wore black dress trousers and a white fitted shirt and there was a scowl on his lips and his eyes were narrowed, as if warning the photographer off.

She accidentally clicked on his profile, but there was only his pseudonym there.

Signor Louis Dupont.
VVIP

So, he was very, *very* important.

And in the box where normally a guest's requests were noted there was instead a direction.

All queries and requests to be directed to Francesca.
All hours.

'Is everything okay, Antonietta?'

She turned to the sound of Francesca's voice and saw she was chatting with Tony.

'Of course. I was just about to make a note regarding a guest but I'm not able to fill it in.'

'Because all Signor Dupont's requests are to be relayed first to *me*,' said Francesca.

'He didn't even *try* one of my pastries?' Tony was aghast when he saw that the trolley had been returned untouched.

Francesca, of course, thought she should have done better. 'You should have left a selection for him to nibble on.'

'He made himself very clear,' Antonietta said, blushing a bit as she did so, knowing that Rafe's lack of compliments to the chef would not go down well. 'I was just about to make a note—he has asked that the chef…' she hesitated and slightly rephrased Rafe's message '…should please not add anything to his order.'

Even that did not go down well.

Tony flounced off and she later found out from Vincenzo, the head of PR, that he had been discovered in tears.

'You know how temperamental Tony is,' he scolded her. 'And he's especially upset today because the Christmas rosters are out. Could you not at least have diluted such a prominent guest's criticism?'

'But I *did* dilute it,' Antonietta said. 'Anyway, I thought Tony was happy to be working on Christmas Day.'

Vincenzo just huffed off, leaving Antonietta wondering what on earth she'd said wrong this time. Still, there wasn't time to dwell, and for the rest of the day she worked with Chi-Chi. Or rather Antonietta worked while Chi-Chi did the *slowly-slowly.*

The *slowly-slowly* was a way to look busy while getting precisely nothing done, and Chi-Chi had perfected it. She had even tried to share her method with Antonietta.

'You can doze in the cleaning room, but keep some dusters on your lap, so that if Francesca pops her head in you can look as if you're in the middle of folding them,' Chi-Chi had explained when Antonietta had first started working there. 'But never cross your legs while you sleep or it will leave a red mark on your calf, and Francesca will be able to tell you've been in there for ages.'

'I don't want a bar of it,' Antonietta had told her.

She had known Chi-Chi her whole life, but she wasn't a friend, exactly, just someone she knew and, unfortunately, with whom she now worked. Chi-Chi's aim in life was to find a husband and do as little as she could get away with in the meantime. Once, Antonietta had actually seen her dozing on her arm as she supposedly cleaned a mirror, only to suddenly spring into action when Antonietta made her presence known!

'I saw your *papà* yesterday,' Chi-Chi said as she ate one of the turn-down chocolates while Antonietta dusted. 'He couldn't stop and speak for long, though, but he said he was busy getting things ready for the Christmas Eve bonfire. Will you be going?' she enquired, oh, so innocently.

'Of course,' Antonietta said. 'The fire in the village square is a tradition. Why wouldn't I go?'

Chi-Chi shrugged and helped herself to another chocolate. 'What is he like?' she asked.

'My *papà*?' Antonietta said, pretending she had no idea to whom Chi-Chi was referring.

'No, silly! The new man who is staying in the August Suite. I wonder what his real name is? He must be important. I have never seen so much security.'

'*All* our guests are important,' Antonietta said, refusing to be drawn.

Still, at the mention of the August Suite, and not for the first time, Antonietta glanced at her pager. But, no, Rafe had not paged her. Nor, when she checked, had he made any requests for in-suite dining. In fact later that afternoon she found out that his nurse had been given her marching orders for daring to make an unscheduled check on her patient.

Rafe had clearly meant what he'd said about not wanting to be disturbed.

At the end of her shift, as she walked back to her little cottage, Antonietta found she was glancing up in the direction of the August Suite. It was too far away for her to tell if he was on the balcony, but she wondered about him, wondered how he had spent his day and how he was.

For the first time ever Antonietta truly wondered about a man…

CHAPTER TWO

THE CHRISTMAS ROSTER was definitely the main topic of conversation over the next couple of days.

Antonietta was training in the Oratory, which was unusually quiet, but whenever she entered the staffroom it was all that was being discussed.

'It's not fair,' Chi-Chi huffed. 'Even Greta has got Christmas off and she only started three months ago.'

'She has children, though,' Antonietta pointed out.

'How come *you* are off, Vincenzo?'

'Because I live in Florence, and if I am to spend any time with my family then I need adequate time to get there.'

'But it is the Old Monastery's first Christmas,' Chi-Chi said. 'Surely the head of PR should be here and tweeting…or whatever it is you do.'

'I do rather more than play on my phone,' Vincenzo said, and then looked to Antonietta. 'How are things in the Oratory?'

'Quiet…' Antonietta sighed as she peeled the lid off a yoghurt. 'It's fully booked for next week, but the place was dead yesterday and it's almost empty today. I think people must be saving up their treatments for Christmas.'

She looked up as Francesca came to the door.

'Ah, there you are Antonietta. Could I ask you to service Signor Dupont's suite? I know you are meant to be doing your training in the Oratory today—'

'Of course,' Antonietta said, and went to get up.

'Finish your lunch first,' Francesca said. 'He has asked that it be serviced at one o'clock.'

'I'm glad she asked you and not me,' Chi-Chi said, the very second Francesca had gone. 'I've been working there the past couple of days, and he might be important, but he's also mean.'

'Mean?' Antonietta frowned.

'He told me to refrain from speaking while I do my work.'

'Well, I expect he has a headache,' Antonietta said, without adding that *she* certainly did when Chi-Chi was around.

Vincenzo looked at the time and then stood and brushed off his suit, smoothing his already immaculate red hair in the mirror before heading back.

'For someone so vain, you'd think he would have noticed that he's putting on weight,' Chi-Chi said the moment he was gone. 'His jacket doesn't even do up any more.'

'Leave him alone,' Antonietta snapped.

But Chi-Chi would not, and carried on with her grumbling. 'He's only got Christmas off because he's a manager.'

'No.' Antonietta shook her head. 'Francesca is working. I'd better go.'

'But you've barely sat down.'

She was happy to get up. Antonietta was more than a little bit fed up with Chi-Chi's rather grating nature.

'I need to get the linen ready to take up to the August Suite.'

Fetching the linen was one of Antonietta's favourite tasks. Here at the Old Monastery the linen was tailor-made for each bed and was washed and line dried without a hint of bleach.

Antonietta breathed in the scent of fresh laundry as she walked in. Vera, who worked there, must be on her lunch, so Antonietta selected crisp linen and then walked across the stunning grounds.

A guest who had just arrived that morning had told her that it had been raining and grey in Rome when they'd left. Here, though, the sky was blue, and it was a little brisk and chilly, with cold nights.

The guard checked her ID and actually addressed her. 'He will be back by two, so please make sure you are done and out by then.'

'Certainly.'

Given that it took well over an hour to service the August Suite to standard, guests often went for a stroll, or down to the Oratory for a treatment, or to the restaurant while the maids worked. Usually she was relieved when the guests were out, but today she felt a stab of disappointment that she chose not to dwell on.

Of course she knocked before entering anyway, and when there was no answer she let herself in and stood for a moment, looking around. The place was a little chaotic, and she was wondering where to start when someone came in from the balcony.

Certainly she had not been expecting to see *him*.

'Buongiorno,' she said, and then immediately lost her tongue, for Rafe was dressed in black running shorts and nothing else.

'Buongiorno.' He returned the greeting, barely looking over. 'I'll be out of your way soon,' he added.

Indeed, Rafe had fully intended to go for a run—his first since the accident. But now he glanced over and recognised the maid from the fog of his first morning here. 'You've had some days off?'

'No,' Antonietta said. 'I haven't had any days off.'

'So why did they send me Chi-Chi?' he drawled, and rolled his eyes.

Antonietta almost smiled, but quickly recovered, because even if Chi-Chi drove her insane she would not discuss her colleague with a guest. Instead she answered as she headed into the bedroom. 'I've been working in the Oratory.'

She paused for a second to let him speak, as she should any guest, but truly she wanted to flee, for her cheeks were on fire and she hoped that he had not noticed. He did not reply.

'I hope you have a pleasant day,' she said.

'Thank you.'

Antonietta put down the list that she always worked from and immediately started stripping the vast walnut bed. She worked quickly, but the exertion was less out of necessity and more to match her heartbeat, which had tripped into a rapid rhythm at the sight of him semi-naked. And when he came into the bedroom to collect his trainers she had to force herself not to look—or rather not to stand there and simply gape.

'You work in the Oratory?' he checked. 'So you are a therapist?'

His voice caught her unawares; for she had not expected the terse gentleman she had met a few days ago to initiate a conversation.

'I'm training to be one,' Antonietta said, and glanced up from the bed.

And then it ceased being a glance, for she met his eyes and the world and its problems seemed for a moment to disappear.

'You look better,' she commented, when usually she would not, but the words had just tumbled out.

'I'm feeling a lot better,' he agreed. 'Although I still look as if I've been paint-bombed.'

She couldn't help but smile, for indeed he did. Those bruises were a riot of colour now, from blue to brown right through to a vivid pink, and they were spread across the left side of his torso and down to his shoulder and arm, and there were savage lines across his shoulder. Rafe's left eye looked as if he was wearing violet eyeshadow.

Yet he wore it well.

In fact, paint-bombed or not, Rafe looked stunning.

And as her eyes briefly travelled over his body, to take in his comment, she found that they wanted to linger on the long, yet muscular arms, and on his broad chest with just a smattering of black hair. More, she found that they lingered on his flat stomach. It was not bruised, so there was no real reason to look there. But Antonietta just found that she did, and a glimpse of that line of black hair had her already hot cheeks reddening as if scalded.

She wanted to ask, *What happened to you?*

Were those bruises from a fight? Or had he been in an accident? For once she wanted to know more, and yet it was not her place to ask.

'I shan't be long,' Rafe said, though usually he did not explain himself to maids, or even particularly notice that they were near.

Crossing the room, he took a seat by the bed she was making and bent over to lace his trainers.

Antonietta did her best to ignore him and not to look at his powerful back and the stretch of his trapezius muscles as he leant forward. Never had her fingers ached to touch so. To reach out with her newly trained therapist's fingers and relax the taut flesh beneath. Only she was self-aware enough to know that that kind of desire had precisely nothing to do with her line of work. He was so very male, and she was so very aware of that fact in a way she had never been until now.

Confused by this new feeling he aroused, Antonietta hurriedly looked away and resumed making the bed. But as she was fitting a sheet he must have caught the scent, and he made a comment.

'The sheets smell of summer.'

Antonietta nodded as she tucked it in. 'They smell of the Silibri sun. All the linen here is line-dried.'

'What about when it rains?'

'The stocks are plentiful—you have to make hay when the sun shines,' Antonietta said. 'Nico, the owner—'

'I know Nico.'

Rafe's interruption said a lot. Nico was prominent, and Rafe had not said I know *of* Nico, or I have *heard* of him. And then he elaborated more. 'It was he who suggested that I come to Silibri to recover.'

That admission made her a little more open to revealing something of herself. 'Aurora, his wife, is my best friend.'

'You are chalk and cheese.'

'Yes…' Antonietta smiled. 'I am drab in comparison.'

'Drab?'

'Sorry,' she said, assuming he didn't know that word. 'I meant…'

'I know what you meant—and, no, you are not.'

Rafe met a lot of people, and had an innate skill that enabled him to sum them up quickly and succinctly.

Yesterday's maid: slovenly.

The concierge, Pino, who had this morning suggested a running route: wise.

His assessments were rapid, and seldom wrong, and as he looked over to the maid he recalled asking her name that first morning. That morning he had not been able to sum *her* up in one word.

Admittedly, he had been concussed, and not at his best, but today he was much better. So he looked at those sad eyes, and, no, he still could not isolate that word.

Their conversation paused, and yet it did not end, for instead of heading out of the balcony and down the private steps to the grounds below he watched as, having made the bed, she headed to an occasional table, where she picked up her notepad and ticked off her list.

'So you are training as a therapist?'

'Yes,' she nodded. 'Although I'm not allowed to be let loose unsupervised on the guests yet. Well, I can give manicures, but that is all.'

'I *loathe* manicures.'

There were two types of men who had manicures, Antonietta had learnt. Those who chose to and those who had been born to. He had been born to, she was quite, quite sure.

She resisted the urge to walk over and examine his hands, but instead looked down at them… Yes, they were exquisite, long-fingered, with very neat, beautifully manicured nails.

'I find sitting there boring.'

'Then why bother?' Antonietta asked, and then pulled back the conversation. 'I'm sorry—that was personal.'

'Not at all,' Rafe said. 'I ask myself the same thing.'

'You could always listen to a podcast while

your nails are being done,' Antonietta suggested.

'Ah, but then I wouldn't get to speak with you.'

It was a silly little joke but she smiled.

The girl with the saddest eyes smiled, and when she did she looked glorious, Rafe thought. Her black eyes sparkled and her full red lips revealed very white teeth. She had a beautiful mouth, Rafe thought, and watched it as she responded to his light jest.

'I would not be allowed to treat a guest in the August Suite.'

He was about to say *What a pity*, but he rather sensed that that would have her scuttling behind the wall she had erected, which was just starting to inch down.

She rather fascinated him, and it was a relief to focus on their gentle conversation rather than deal with the problems he must face. He had intended to go for a run, just to clear his head. Yet instead he carried on chatting as she worked her way through the suite.

'You grew up here?' he asked.

'Yes, I left a few years ago.'

'For how long?'

'Five years,' Antonietta said. 'And though it was wonderful, I came to realise that you cannot drift for ever. Home is home—though it is very different now, and the hotel has changed things. There are more people, more work…'

'Is that why you came back?'

'No,' Antonietta said, and cut that line of conversation stone-cold dead.

It usually took an hour and fifteen minutes to service the suite to standard. Today it took a little longer, although they did not talk non-stop, just made gentle conversation as Antonietta got on with her work, diligently ticking off items in turn to ensure that nothing had been missed.

'Do you have family here?' Rafe asked, curious despite himself.

'Yes.'

Again she closed the topic, and headed into the lounge and dining area. There had been no fire lit last night, and no meal taken, but she dusted the gleaming table, then topped up the cognac decanter and replaced the glasses.

Tick.

He was leaning on the doorframe, watching her. Usually to have a guest watching her so overtly would be unsettling, yet it didn't feel that way with Rafe. She found him relaxing. Oh, her heart was in her throat, and beating way too fast, but that was for other reasons entirely.

She liked it that he did not demand elaboration. So much so that as she put the stopper in the decanter she revealed to him a little of her truth.

'We are not really speaking.'

'That must be hard.'

'Yes.'

The candles in the heavy candelabra were new, and didn't need replacing.

Tick.

She checked that the lighter worked.

Tick.

But she paused for a moment and wondered how used to luxury he must be not to light them each night. Not to need the stunning suite bathed in candle and firelight.

'The August Suite is my favourite,' Antonietta admitted. 'You should use these candles. I am sure it would look beautiful.'

'I'll keep that in mind.'

'I mean…' She was flustered, for she was not used to idle conversation. 'I've always wondered what it must look like.'

'I'll bear that in mind,' Rafe said again, and this time she flushed. 'Which is your favourite view?' he asked.

'The one from the dining room. From there you can see the valley.'

'Show me.'

As easily as that, he joined her at the window.

'When I left,' Antonietta said, 'that whole stretch of valley was black and scorched from wild fires.' She pointed to a large clearing atop a hillside. 'My family's property is up there.'

'Was it razed in the fires?'

'No, the fires stopped short of Silibri, but in the next village, where I also have family, there was a lot of damage. It's hard now to remember that it was so dead and black. I came back in spring, for Nico and Aurora's wedding, and the whole valley was a riot of colour. I have never seen it so alive. I find the view soothing. It reminds me that, as terrible as the fires were, they were good for the land.'

'So you stayed on after the wedding?'

'No,' Antonietta said. 'I went to Rome for a year, but I wanted to be back here for Christmas.' She gave him a tight smile. Certainly, she was not going to reveal that right now a happy family Christmas was looking less and less likely. 'I had better get on.'

'Of course.'

Nothing was left unchecked.

No cushion left unturned or unplumped.

And still Rafe did not go for his run. Instead he made a couple of phone calls, and it turned her insides to liquid to hear his deep voice flow in the language she loved.

'You are French?' she asked, after the second call had ended, although usually she would not pry.

'No,' Rafe said. 'But it is the language of my home.'

'Oh?'

'Tulano,' he added. 'It is between Italy and France...'

'I know where it is,' Antonietta said. 'I visited there once. Only briefly, though.'

His eyes narrowed a touch. In truth, Rafe did not believe she didn't know who he was. The maid yesterday had slipped up and called him by his full first name—Rafael—and the concierge had done the same when recommending a trail to run.

Soon, he was sure, his location would be leaked and the press would be here. The brief respite from the world would be over.

He asked her a question. 'Do you speak French?'

'Some—although not as much as I would like. I was there for four years,' she said, and then switched to French and told him that his Italian was better than her French. *'Votre Italien est meilleur que mon Français.'*

And he responded. *'Ta voix est délicieuse dans les deux langues.'*

She had been away from France for over a year, and it took her a moment to translate it, but as she did a heated blush crept up her neck.

Had he just said that her voice was delightful in both languages?

Were they flirting?

And if they were then why wasn't she halting it?

Why wasn't she running for cover, as she usually did whenever a man, let alone a guest, got a little too close?

Only Rafe wasn't too close for comfort. And Antonietta looked at the eyes that held hers as she responded. *'Ainsi est le tien.'*

So is yours.

It was the tiniest nod to his effect on her, and yet it felt rather huge to Antonietta.

There was another phone call for Rafe, and this time he answered in Italian, taking it out on the balcony.

Though she did not eavesdrop, his low voice reached her and it was clear that he was speaking with Nico. She felt a little flip of disappointment when she heard him state that he would not be staying for much longer.

The call ended and she looked over to where he sat, his long legs stretched out on another chair, his dark eyes scanning the grounds as a prisoner's might, as if looking for a way to escape. She could almost feel his restlessness,

Antonietta thought as she headed out onto the balcony to finish her work.

'That was Nico,' he said, though he had absolutely no need to do so. 'Checking that I'm being looked after. He suggests that I take a wander into the village.'

'There are nice cafés there,' Antonietta said, and deliberately kept her voice casual. But there was a flip in her stomach at the thought he might be bored. 'Have you been down to the temple ruins?'

'No—that is where Pino suggested I ran.'

'And the ocean is glorious,' Antonietta said, and then stopped herself. It was not her job to sell the village to a reluctant guest.

'You live in the village?'

'No. Nico and Aurora have been very good to me. They knew coming back would be difficult…' She briefly closed her eyes, instantly regretting revealing so much, and then hurriedly spoke on. 'So they gave me a cottage in the grounds.' She pointed in the vague direction of the helipad, over to the far side of the Old Monastery.

'That must be very...' He hesitated, not wanting to say *isolated.*

Already, for Rafe, no matter how spacious and luxurious the August Suite, no matter how glorious the grounds, cabin fever was seriously hitting. This place really was in the middle of nowhere, and he'd been considering checking out later today.

Yet he was starting to change his mind.

Rafe wanted more of her smile, of her conversation—much, much more of her.

It was not as simple as that, though.

If their relationship were to evolve, then she needed to sign a non-disclosure agreement. She would have to be be vetted by his security staff and her phone would be confiscated before they so much as went out for dinner.

It could be no other way.

Yes, he had had a couple of relationships without such arrangements, but they had been with titled women and potential wives. This Antonietta could never be that. And he must test the waters to find out how she felt.

'That must be very quiet,' Rafe said.

'No,' Antonietta refuted as she watered the

jasmine. 'I can hear the waves, and I am by the helipad so there are helicopters coming and going. Believe me, they are *loud* when they're overhead. But most of the time it is nice and peaceful.'

'Still…' Rafe said, and his voice was low as his eyes commanded hers to meet his. 'One can have too much tranquillity.'

Their eyes met and his words travelled through her like a current. Looking hastily away, she saw the slight shake of her hand as she watered the flowers and felt the devilish pull of his smooth voice.

Something told Antonietta that her response mattered, for his statement had felt like a question. More…it had felt like an invitation.

One she rapidly chose to decline.

'I am all for tranquillity,' Antonietta said rather crisply.

And instead of meeting his eyes, or thinking of something witty to add, she went back to her list and added a tick.

The flowers were watered, his suite was done and she gave him a smile—only this time, Rafe noted, it was a guarded one.

'I hope the rest of your day is pleasant,' Antonietta said, and let herself out, exhaling a long-held breath once the door between them was closed. She felt a little giddy.

When she entered the elevator to go down, she walked straight into Francesca.

'There you are! What on earth took you so long?' Francesca scolded the very second she clapped eyes on Antonietta, but then she must have regretted her tone, because she said, 'Oh, Antonietta, I apologise. I forgot that Chi-Chi has been working there for the past couple of days. The place must have been in disarray.'

It was Antonietta who was in disarray, though. Had Rafe been suggesting something?

There was little she could pin on his words, and yet there had been a wicked edge in their delivery—she was almost sure of it.

But she'd had no experience with men.

Not good ones, anyway.

For all Sylvester's attempts, his kisses and gropes had never, not once, made her feel the way that Rafe did with just his voice, just his eyes…

She was not only inexperienced in the kissing department, but in the flirting one too. And they *had* been flirting. Or was she romanticising things? Antonietta pondered as she went about her day. Certainly she was innocent, but she wasn't naïve, and she knew from her work in other hotels that Rafe might have been suggesting *'in-room service'*, so to speak.

She managed a soft laugh at that thought, for if that were the case Rafe was certainly wide of the mark.

And yet he had buoyed her up in a way she could not properly explain…

CHAPTER THREE

RAFE HAD BUOYED her up. The day felt brighter for the time she had spent with him.

And the night felt not so long, nor as dark, and Antonietta awoke the next morning with delicious anticipation.

Yes, even the *prospect* of seeing Rafe buoyed her up.

So much so that she decided to stroll into the village and do her shopping before her shift started.

In so many ways it was wonderful to be back. As Antonietta had explained to Rafe, when she had left Silibri it had been after a summer of fierce wild fires and the mountains and trees had been charred and black.

In fact the village had been slowly dying even before she was born, with shops and cafés closing and the youth moving on. Now, though, with the monastery refurbished, there was new growth all around. The trees were lush and there were winter wild flowers lining the roads. The village itself was thriving. Its produce and wares were now in demand, and the cafés were busy and vibrant.

She had already done some of her Christmas shopping—as well as presents for her parents and brother there was a lipstick for Aurora, which she bought faithfully each year. Just because her friend was newly rich, and could afford a lifetime's supply of the vibrant red cosmetic, some things never changed.

Some things *did* change, though. Aurora was married now, and so Antonietta bought some chocolate for Nico at one of the craft stalls in the village square. And not just any chocolate. Hand-made Modica chocolate, which was so exquisite that even a man who had everything could never have enough.

Bizarrely, she thought of Rafe.

Or perhaps not so bizarrely. Because she had been thinking of him on and off since the previous day. More accurately, he had been popping into her thoughts since the day they had met.

'Could I get the coffee flavour, too, please?'

Antonietta said impulsively to the stallholder—and then jumped when she heard her name.

'Antonietta?'

It was Pino.

'Did I catch you buying me a gift?' he teased, when he saw her reddening cheeks.

'No, no…' Antonietta smiled back and then glanced at his shopping bag, which was empty. She knew that Pino was just killing time. 'Are you on a day off?'

'Yes, though I thought you were working?'

'Not till midday. But Francesca wants me to go in a little early. No doubt because of our esteemed guest.' She felt her cheeks go a little more pink.

'That's probably it.' Pino rolled his eyes. 'I heard he has asked not to have Chi-Chi service his suite again.'

'Really?' Antonietta's eyes widened. 'Why?'

'I thought you didn't like to gossip?' Pino teased.

'I don't,' Antonietta said, and hurriedly changed the subject. 'Now, I have to choose *two* presents for Gabe—it is his first birthday next week, and then Christmas too.'

Pino was delighted to help, and soon they had a little wooden train for him, as well as a cute outfit, and Pino suggested they go for coffee.

'I don't have time,' Antonietta said, which wasn't quite true.

The sweet, spicy scent of *buccellato*—an Italian Christmas cake—wafted through a nearby café, and though she was tempted Antonietta was too nervous about bumping into her family to stop there for coffee and cake.

Instead, having said goodbye to Pino, she decided that she would bake her own, and headed into the village store. There she chose the figs and almonds that she needed to make the cake, and added a few other things to her basket before lining up to pay.

The shopkeeper was awkward with her, and did not make eye contact—and then Antonietta found out why.

'Stronza!'

The insult came from behind, and Antonietta did not need to turn her head to know that the word was aimed at her. She had been called worse on previous trips to the shops. Steadfastly, she did not turn around, and though she was tempted to walk out without her groceries, she held her ground.

Another insult was hurled. *'Puttana!'*

They all assumed there must have been another man for her to have run out on Sylvester, or that she had been sleeping with all and sundry in her years away.

Let them think what they choose, Antonietta told herself as she paid.

But as she picked up her bag she saw that it was Sylvester's aunt who was taunting her.

Antonietta said nothing. She just did her best to leave with her head held high—or not quite high, but nor was she head down and fleeing as she had previously. She was determined not to let the incident ruin her day.

But it was about to get worse.

Her parents were walking arm in arm towards her, and both were startled when they saw her.

'Mamma!' Antonietta called.

But together they looked away and crossed to the other side of the street. For Antonietta it was a new version of hell. That they should cross the road to avoid her was not only painful and humiliating, it made her angry too, and hurt words tumbled out.

'I tried to tell you, Mamma!'

Her voice was strangled then, but the words were true, for she *had* tried to reveal her fears about Sylvester to her mother. Antonietta watched as Tulia Ricci's shoulders stiffened. She stopped walking, and slowly turned around.

'You *know* I tried to tell you.'

'Antonietta.' Her father spoke then. 'What are you doing back here?'

And as she saw his cold expression she wondered the very same thing.

It was Antonietta who walked off, refusing to cry.

Even at the hotel she felt an anger building that was unfamiliar to her.

But her shift would start soon, and Antonietta decided she could not think about her family situation *and* do her work, so she fought to set it aside. Tonight she would examine it. Tonight she would sit down and decide whether to stay long enough to complete her training, to give them a chance for a Christmas reunion, but she would not think of it now.

She changed quickly into her uniform and then, with her heart fluttering in her chest and her breath coming too shallow and too fast, she crossed the monastery grounds.

Antonietta was usually a full fifteen minutes early for work, but so shaken was she by the morning's events that she got there only just in time.

'*There* you are!' Francesca said by way of greeting. 'Signor Dupont has requested that his suite be serviced at midday, when he is out.'

Antonietta nodded and made her way up to the suite. After knocking and getting no answer, she let herself in. There was the scent of him in the air, but not his presence, and she was relieved to be alone and not have to make small talk. She set to work, ticking things off her list, trying to banish all thoughts of this morning.

Except Antonietta could not.

As she smoothed the sheets on the bed all she could see was the sight of her parents, crossing the street to avoid her. She plumped the pillow but found she was crushing it between her hands as the tears started to come thick and fast.

And they were *angry* tears!

She had come here to make amends.

To say sorry to her parents for not marrying a man who had treated her less than gently. A man who had tried to force her to do *that* more than once.

She had held on to her anger for so long, but it was more than seeping out now, and she buried her face in the pillow and let out a muffled scream.

'Agh!'

It felt good.

So good that she did it again.

'Agh!'

And again.

That was how Rafe found her.

He had finally gone for a run—in part to avoid *her*, for such was his cabin fever that he was getting a little too interested in a certain maid.

And that would *never* do.

However, he had not been for a run since his accident, and his endurance was not quite what it had been. He would soon get it back, he told himself, and the next run would be longer.

He made his way up the stone stairs to the private beach entrance of the balcony.

And then he saw her shouting into a pillow.

Rafe did not get involved with the dramas of maids.

Ever.

But when she stopped shouting into the pillow and sobbed into it instead, something twisted inside him even though generally tears did not move him.

She was not crying for an audience; he was aware that he was witnessing something private that she would rather no one saw.

Indeed, Antonietta was mortified when she removed the pillow and saw Rafe.

He was breathing heavily from running, and he looked displeased.

'I apologise,' Antonietta said immediately, for an esteemed guest did not need anything other than quiet efficiency. She wiped her cheeks with her hands and started to peel off the pillowcase as her words tumbled out. 'I thought you were out.'

‘It’s fine.’ Rafe shrugged.

‘I ran into my parents…’ She attempted to explain. ‘They crossed the street to avoid me.’

‘I see.’ Rafe tried to remain unmoved. No, he did *not* get involved with the dramas of maids.

‘I can send someone else up…’ Antonietta hiccoughed, frantically trying to regain control. Except her tears would not stop.

‘There’s no need for that,’ Rafe said. ‘Carry on.’

‘But, as you can see, I can’t stop crying…’

‘I said,’ Rafe snapped, ‘carry on.’

And though she did carry on with her work, she found that the tears carried on too, and the anger did not abate.

No pillow was left unthumped!

He ignored her.

Well, not quite. At one point, when anger gave way to sorrow, he gave a slight roll of his eyes and handed his weeping maid a handkerchief.

She carried on with her work.

She just dribbled tears, and she was so grateful for his lack of words, that there was no attempt at comfort, for there was nothing he could say.

She would never have her family back. Of that Antonietta was certain. And it was there in the August Suite that she finally mourned them. Oh, there was no howling. Antonietta just quietly let the tears roll.

Rafe did not involve himself.

He would have liked to have a shower, given he had just been for a run, except he did not want to have a shower while the weeping maid was here.

Of course he could dismiss her.

And yet he did not.

Instead Rafe stood on the balcony and looked out towards the temple ruins, wondering about his teary maid.

He recalled the slight triumph he had felt when she'd smiled, and he found he would like her to smile again.

In turn, she liked the silence he gave her. It did not feel as if she was crying alone, as she had done so many times. And neither did she feel patronised, for there had been no *there, there* or invasive questions.

He let her be, and finally she was done with both her work and her tears.

Every last thing on her list was ticked off and Antonietta felt surprisingly calm as she gathered her things and finally addressed Rafe. 'I am finished.'

'Perhaps before you go down you should go and splash your face with cold water…take a moment.'

She did as she was told, appalled to see her swollen eyes and red nose, but she appreciated the opportunity to calm down, and retied her hair before heading out.

'If you need anything else, please page me.'

'I shan't,' Rafe said, but then he reconsidered, for Antonietta really was proving to be the brightest part of his day… But, no, he would not make up reasons to call her. 'Are you working tomorrow?'

'Just a half-day,' Antonietta said. 'Then I have a day off.'

'Well, I might see you tomorrow, then?'

He hoped so.

So did she.

'Thank you,' Antonietta said as she turned to leave, instead of the other way around.

'No problem.'

Except there clearly was.

'Antonietta.'

He called her name as she headed for the door. And his summons hit her deep and low, and the word felt like a hand coming down on her shoulder. How could the sound of her own name make her tremble and feel almost scared to turn around?

Or rather *nervous* to turn around.

Slowly she did turn, and she knew in that second that she was not scared or even nervous to face him. She was fighting her own desire.

In the room behind him she could see the vast bed, and she wanted to lie with him on white sheets that smelt of summer. To know the bliss not just of *a* man, but of *him*.

Rafe.

Whoever he was.

'Yes?' Her voice sounded all wrong. It was too breathless and low and so she said it again—except it came out no better, was a mere croak. 'Yes?'

Rafe rarely—extremely rarely—did not know how to proceed. Not only did he not get involved with maids' dramas, neither did he take maids to bed.

Added to that, she had been crying for the best part of an hour. He never took advantage.

Yet the air was charged. She looked as if he'd just kissed her, and he could feel the energy between them and her increasing awareness of him.

His sad maid looked exactly as she might if he had her pressed against the wall.

'I could have one of my security detail come and speak with you?'

'Why would they need to speak with me?' She frowned, trying to untangle her thoughts from his words. Trying to remind herself that she was at work. 'Is there a problem with security in the suite?' She was desperately trying to hold a normal conversation as her body screamed for contact with his. 'If that's the case I can let Francesca know.'

She knew nothing about his ways, Rafe realised.

'It's fine,' Rafe said. 'My mistake.'

'Mistake?' Antonietta checked, and he could see that her eyes were perturbed, that she assumed she'd said something wrong.

But she'd said everything right.

For this was far more straightforward and yet way more complicated than a contracted affair.

This was pure, unadulterated lust.

From both of them.

And he actually believed now that she had no idea who he was.

Crown Prince Rafael of Tulano.

CHAPTER FOUR

'RAFAEL, BY ALL accounts you could have been killed.'

Rafe had spoken with his father since the accident, but the King hadn't called to enquire as to his health. 'Had you died as my sole heir,' the King continued in reprimand, 'the country would have been plunged into turmoil and well you know it. Did you think of that as you hurled yourself down the mountain?'

'Actually,' Rafe responded, 'I did.'

As he had fallen—as he had realised the seriousness of the unfolding incident—it had dawned on him that this might well be it and he had thought of his country. He had thought of the royal lineage shifting to his father's brother, of his idle, ignorant, spoiled cousins ruling the land that Rafe loved and their undoubted glee that finally the reckless Crown Prince had succumbed.

'Thank God it has been kept out of the press,' the King went on. 'Our people have thankfully been spared from knowing how close this country came *again* to losing its Crown Prince. But it is not enough, Rafe. You need to temper your ways.'

'Then give me more responsibility. Transition some of your power to me.'

It was the same argument they had had of old. Rafe was a natural-born leader who had been raised to be King and already wanted a more prominent role than merely making staged appearances. He did not want to be a pin-up prince; he wanted active power and to be a voice amongst world leaders, yet his father resisted.

'You know the answer to that,' the King responded tartly.

Yes.

Marriage.

And a suitable bride chosen for him by his father the King.

Rafe did not trust his father with that decision. After all, he had witnessed first-hand the hell of his parents' *suitable* marriage.

There was a reason that Rafe was the only heir to the Tulano throne—after he had been born his father had resumed his rakish ways.

His mother understood her duty to the country, and the impact of a divorce, and so it had never been considered. Emotions and feelings were rarely taken into account at the palace. The King and Queen's marriage was a working relationship only. The Queen met with the King daily, accompanied him on formal occasions and hosted functions with grace, but she had her own wing at the palace and had long ago removed herself from his bed.

And there was no 'family life' as such. Rafe had been raised by palace nannies and had later attended boarding school.

No, there was nothing Rafe had witnessed that endeared him to marriage or to the idea of starting a family of his own.

'I expect you back here on Christmas Eve,' the King said. 'Preferably in one piece and without scandal attached. Do you think you can possibly manage that?'

Rafe wasn't sure.

As luxurious as the Old Monastery was, he

was already climbing the walls and ready to check out. In fact, he had been about to call Nico to thank him for his hospitality when the call from the palace had come.

'I shall put your mother on.'

To his mother, he was an afterthought. She would never think to call him herself. Instead, when he spoke to his father, she occasionally deigned to come to the phone.

As he awaited the Queen, Rafe decided that if he was going to hide from the public eye then it might as well be on a yacht. Somewhere warm, with requisite beauties. The Caribbean was calling, Rafe thought as he heard his mother's icy tone.

'Rafe.'

'Mother.'

'What a foolish waste of a great ruler it would have been had you been killed.'

'What a foolish waste it is now,' Rafe responded. 'I am told I'm expected to return for Christmas to inspect an army I can no longer fight alongside because you both deem it too dangerous. Perhaps the balcony I have to stand on and wave from is too high? Too much of a risk.'

'Don't be facetious.'

'I am not,' Rafe responded. 'I am bored with being an idle prince...'

'Then act accordingly and you will be given the responsibility you crave.'

Marriage.

All conversations, all rows, all roads led to that. And the pressure did not come solely from his family but from the people, who longed to see their reckless Prince settled.

'I don't require a wife in order to make decisions.'

'You need to temper your ways. At least in the eyes of the public.'

'So as long as I am discreet I can carry on as before?' Rafe checked, and there was no disguising the disgust in his tone.

But his mother was unmoved. 'You have your father's heart, Rafe,' Queen Marcelle responded matter-of-factly. 'No one expects you to be faithful—we all know that your love is reserved for your country. And that country wants to see its Prince married and with heirs.'

'I decide when.'

'Fine,' said his mother. 'Until then, enjoy waving from the balcony!'

They had had this discussion on many occasions, though the news that he could take mistresses, like his father did, was a new development. But not a welcome one. Rafe admired many things about the King, but abhorred plenty.

He had the last word, Rafe knew. But he could not force him to marry.

And yet he could feel the pressure to conform tightening.

Rafe had not been lying when he'd told the King that his country had been on his mind as he'd fallen. Perhaps it was time to take a break from his partying ways, for Rafe was surprised to find himself growing tired of them.

Back on the balcony, he was thinking of one particular beauty. It was too confined here. That must be the reason why his thoughts had again wandered to Antonietta, for usually he allowed himself to get close to no one.

Her tears had moved him.

He wanted to spoil her. He wanted that smile he had seen so briefly to return to her lips.

One more night in Silibri, Rafe told himself.

And he would not be spending it alone.

CHAPTER FIVE

WHO WAS HE?

For the first time Antonietta truly wanted to know more about a guest—or rather, she corrected herself, about a man.

Her no-gossip rule wasn't serving her well now.

But the Internet service in her tiny cottage really was *terrible*.

To her own slight bemusement, an hour after her shift had ended Antonietta found herself heading out of her cottage and standing on a cliff, typing *Rafe* and *Tulano* into her laptop.

No service.

Agh!

She stomped back to her cottage and told herself she was being ridiculous. Whoever Rafe really was, it was irrelevant, given he'd be gone in a matter of days.

Yet, she wanted to know.

She was too embarrassed to ask Pino, who would generally be her main source of information, having shut down his conversation that first morning. And Chi-Chi, who usually daydreamed aloud about any male she saw as a potential suitor, was unusually quiet. Vincenzo was too discreet.

Oh, how she regretted refusing to let Francesca reveal his identify to her. She could hardly ask her for more information now—it would only raise suspicion. Nico, and in turn Francesca, were very strict about staff keeping a professional distance from their guests.

It was why she was doing so well.

A knock at the door startled her. No one ever came and visited her at the cottage. Well, except for Aurora, but usually she would text to say that she was on her way. Could it be her parents, feeling guilty about avoiding her earlier in the village? Was she finally going to get the Christmas she had craved?

There was a spark of hope as she pulled open the door. But that tiny ray of hope dimmed when she saw who it was.

Rafe!

Actually, it didn't dim. That little spark shrank and regrouped and then reignited, hot, white and blue, as if the collar of a Bunsen burner had been altered.

'Rafe!'

And it was a Rafe she had never seen before. He looked more like the man in the photo attached to his profile except in that he was scowling. In fact, he was smiling, making no attempt to hide his pleasure at her shock.

He wore a dinner suit, and he wore it so very well.

The first time she had seen him he had been rumpled and his hair matted with blood. Now it was black and glossy and brushed back from his elegant face.

There was still a deep bruise on his eyelid, but the swelling had gone, and he was so elegant and commanding, so unexpected and exquisite, that he was simply too much.

'You shouldn't be here,' Antonietta said immediately.

'I didn't see any signs warning me not to trespass.'

'How did you know where I live?'

'Thankfully there is only one cottage near the helipad.' Rafe shrugged. 'Or I might have ended up at Chi-Chi's—I'd never have got out alive…'

Despite herself, Antonietta found that she was laughing at the vision his words created. The most stunning man stood at her door, and instead of being nervous she was laughing!

But she stopped herself. 'I can't invite you in.'

'I'm not asking to be let in,' Rafe responded smoothly. 'I'm inviting you to come out.'

'Out?'

'After the day you've had, I thought you might like a night of being spoiled.'

'I can't be seen in the restaurant with a guest.' Antonietta shook her head, but as one hand went to close the door her other hand resisted and held it part-way open—a kind of push-pull within her as she offered more reasons to say no. 'And I don't want to be seen in the village…'

'So we go further afield,' he said easily. 'My driver is waiting, if a night out appeals…?'

If a night out appeals?

Her mouth gaped at his choice of words. It

more than appealed; pure temptation had come knocking at her door in the delectable shape of Rafe. And yet, as irresistible as his offer was, here came the voice of reason.

He's bored, the voice told her. *You are a mere diversion.*

And the voice became more insistent, rather unkindly pointing out that she was way too inexperienced to handle such prowess and likely it was not just her company he sought.

'I'm not allowed to date guests.'

'Who said anything about a date?'

Those eyes did, Antonietta wanted to respond. They made her feel warm, and important, and deliciously sought after.

He played it down. 'It is dinner at a restaurant. I could use some company, that is all.' He looked at her. 'And so could you. It is my last night in Sicily. It seems a shame to leave without seeing some of it.'

Her heart sank at the news.

She had been told from the very start, even before they had met, when he had been simply Signor Dupont to her, that he undoubtedly would not last until Christmas Eve and would soon leave. Yet he was *Rafe* now, the man who brightened her day, and soon he would be gone.

Was that why she was considering his offer?

'Where?'

'I shall leave that to my driver. We have to try not to be seen, but it shouldn't be a problem…'

Antonietta frowned. Why would he worry about being seen out? She could think of only one thing.

'You don't have a wife?' she hurriedly checked. 'I know it's not a date, but…' Her voice trailed off.

'Antonietta, I don't have a wife, or a girlfriend. It's my parents who want me to lie low.'

His response gave her some relief, but also confused her. Rafe certainly didn't *look* like a man who worried about what his parents thought.

'Will you join me?' he asked.

A night of reheated pizza, ruminating over her parents' actions that morning and regretting her decision not to join this beautifully dizzying man for dinner? Such a night would be spent loathing her decision and her absolute inability to throw caution to the wind.

In fact, it might even become a lifetime of regret.

'Yes,' Antonietta said. 'I would love to join you.'

What were you supposed to wear when the sexiest man alive had arrived on your doorstep with a driver, and was waiting to whisk you to dinner?

Antonietta had but one possibility.

And, just as she had reluctantly handed the fabric over to Aurora, she now almost reluctantly slid the dress on.

Because it changed her.

Aurora was a brilliant seamstress. The silk had been cut on the bias, so the dress was as fluid as water and skimmed her body, enhancing the subtle curves The only issue she had was that it was so strappy it showed her bra, and Antonietta did not possess a strapless one.

Thankfully she was small-breasted, and Aurora had lined the top of the dress, but it still felt a little sinful to head out without one.

There was no time to fuss with her hair, so

she simply brushed it and settled for wearing it down.

The dress needed no heels, but it certainly required lipstick.

Antonietta had no make-up of her own, and so, promising herself she would replenish it, she opened Aurora's Christmas present and painted her mouth crimson.

No, she would not save the dress for her coffin—and yet she felt like a liar as she stared in the mirror, for truly she was not the woman her reflection portrayed. She was not sexy, nor beautiful, Antonietta told herself, even if the dress said that she was.

Oh, but to Rafe she was.

Antonietta could not know the breath of fresh air that she was to him.

'I lied to you,' Rafe said as she approached.

'You *are* married…'

She knew it! He was simply too good to be true.

'No,' Rafe said, 'but this *is* a date, Antonietta.'

Her breath hitched and that flame spread warmth in her chest and down to her stomach.

'This can go nowhere…' he was very direct in telling her there could be no future for them '…but that doesn't change the fact that tonight I would love to get to know you some more.'

Before she responded, Antonietta knew she had to make something very clear. She did not know his motives, and she would not spend the whole night worrying about them, and so she would be upfront.

'I won't sleep with you, Rafe.'

'You would be a very boring dinner companion if you did.'

'I meant—'

'I know what you meant.' He smiled. 'Don't worry. *I* wouldn't sleep with me either—there's far too much paperwork involved.'

'Paperwork?'

'Come on,' he said, without clarifying what he meant, but she was glad she had told him the night would not end in bed, all the same.

He took her hand and led her to the waiting car, and it made her just a little dizzy that part of her didn't want to know that tomorrow she might wake up and think this had all been just a dream. Perhaps it was.

His driver took them through the village, and Antonietta was grateful for the blacked-out windows because of the number of people who turned and looked at the luxurious vehicle. But as they passed the tiny church—the one she failed to turn up to on her wedding day—Rafe must have felt her ripple of tension.

He turned and looked at her. 'Are you okay?' he checked.

'Of course.'

Except she wasn't. Because a short while later they passed her parents' property and she wondered what they would make of her going out on a date with a guest.

'Don't worry about your parents now.'

'How did you know I was thinking of them?'

'You pointed out where they live,' he reminded her. 'Forget about everything,' he told her. 'Tonight we escape.'

Only not quite.

They drove up the winding hillside and then down into the valley, and there was a certain exhilaration that swept through her at leaving the village she knew so well. But when she glanced behind them, the same car that had followed them out of the Old Monastery was still there.

'Are they following us?' Antonietta asked.

'It's just my security.' Rafe shrugged. 'Don't worry about them.'

But she did.

Not just because Rafe came with a full security detail, but because there was clearly more power to him than she could properly define. She felt as if she had run into the night with a giant—and not just in stature. There was an authoritative air to him that she had never encountered before, even in the most esteemed guests, a commanding edge that both enthralled and unnerved her.

Who *was* he?

Less than an hour ago she had been desperate to find out, but now she was scared to know.

'Do you like to dance?' Rafe asked.

'I don't dance,' Antonietta said. 'Well, I *can't* dance,' she admitted, and then frowned as he pressed the intercom and spoke with his driver.

'The lady likes to dance.'

The restaurant he took her to was stunning.

His security team went into the trattoria before them, and she felt a little awkward when they were seated and she saw that the guards had stayed close.

'Do they *have* to be here?' Antonietta checked.

Rafe was so used to them that for a second he was about to ask to whom she referred, but then Antonietta spoke on.

'We're in the middle of nowhere.'

Only it wasn't just for *his* protection that they were close. It was to stop diners taking photos if he was recognised and also, Rafe knew bitterly, to report back to the King.

Rafe lived his life in the presence of staff—maids and aides, advisors and security—and barely noticed them. Yet he could see her discomfort.

'I'll have a word,' Rafe said.

He had several words, and none of them went down very well, for the Crown Prince's behaviour tonight was most irregular.

Still, soon enough they were dining alone.

Wine was poured and Antonietta realised just how hard it was to be in the village day after day after day. Being away from it, she could actually feel the tension leaving, and she let out a sigh as she put down her wine.

'That's better,' Rafe said. 'It's nice to see you looking…'

He didn't really know how to say it—it seemed there was a lightness to her that hadn't been there before. And he felt better being away from the hotel too. It was a relief from the constant weight of planning his next move forward.

'I don't know what to have,' Antonietta admitted, but then her eyes fell on the words 'pistachio pesto' and her mind was made up.

'I've never tried it,' Rafe said.

'Then you don't know what you're missing.' Antonietta smiled.

They ordered their main courses and then, finally alone, they clinked glasses.

'Saluti,' the French-speaking Rafe said.

'Santé!' Antonietta said, and looked him in the eye as they clinked glasses.

He was still looking at her as she took a sip of her drink and then rested back into her seat.

'It is good to be away,' Antonietta admitted. 'It's nice not to be stared at.'

'People were staring when we walked in,' Rafe said. 'Because you look beautiful.'

'Thank you,' Antonietta said. 'It's the dress.'

'Believe me, it's not just the dress,' Rafe said, and he realised he was more relaxed than he had been in a very long while.

It was a gorgeous restaurant, but the atmosphere was peaceful. And Antonietta was right: it was nice not to have his minders so close. Nice to tear bread and dip it in oil and to just… *be*.

Here, she was no longer his chambermaid. Which meant he could ask, 'What happened with your parents?' And she could choose whether or not she answered.

Antonietta looked at this delectable man and, though she would love his take on things, she did not want to bring the mood down. 'I don't want to bore you with it, Rafe.'

'So, give me the short version, then.'

He made her laugh. Oh, there was no *ha-ha-ha*, but his brusque humour teased a single note from her closed throat and stretched her lips to a smile.

He relaxed her. Even while she was nervous and out of her depth, still Rafe's presence somehow eased her soul.

'I was to be married,' Antonietta said. 'I have a very big family, across all the villages, and my father is very well connected…' She stopped herself. 'Sorry, you want the short version.'

'Take as long as you like.'

Her eyes widened, for he sounded as if he meant it. 'I've never really told anyone the whole thing. Then again, I've never had to—everyone already knows…'

'Ah, but do they know *your* version of events?'

'No.' She shook her head and thought for a moment. *'No,'* she said again, for even Aurora had not heard the news from her first-hand.

'It will go no further,' he assured her, 'and I would love to hear it.'

'The day I turned twenty-one I was told that I was to marry my second cousin, Sylvester.'

Antonietta had found that there were generally two reactions to this revelation—a slight grimace of discomfort or a nod of acceptance that said of *course* she should marry into the family, because that was where the money had to stay.

She looked at Rafe to gauge his reaction. There was no grimace and there was no nod. There was just patience.

She looked down. 'At the last minute I decided I couldn't go through with it. I jilted him.'

She dared not look up, but then his hand came across the table and closed around hers.

'Antonietta, can I have the slightly longer version, please?'

She gave a soft laugh, but it was laced with unshed tears—not just because of the subject matter, it was more the bliss of contact, the touch of his skin on hers that somehow cooled her endless scalding shame.

'I should have told him. I know that. Instead I left him standing at the altar. I ran away.'

'In your wedding dress?'

Still he held her hand.

'No. I pulled on some jeans and climbed out of the bedroom window. My father was waiting to take me to the church. By the time he worked out what I had done I was already on the train.'

To Rafe, the waiter coming over with their meals felt like an intrusion, and he wanted to wave him away.

For Antonietta, though, it felt like a reprieve, and her only reluctance at this break in conversation was that their hands had to part.

Then there were flurries of pepper and cheese, and their glasses were topped up, and Rafe could sense her relief not to be talking about herself any more.

He was not used to reticence.

The women he dated—for want of a better word—were only too happy to spend *hours* talking about themselves. Their upcoming photoshoot, their latest role, their clean and green diet, their blah-blah-blah.

And then they would casually ask if he knew so-and-so, which meant could he possibly have a word with them? Not that they wanted favours or anything, they would hastily add.

And then they would sip their thimble of champagne and pretend it had gone to their head, even as they kept all their wits about them, for this was their chance to get ahead, get seen, get a step up on the A-list ladder.

Oh, yes, Rafe knew their game well, because over and over he had allowed them to play it. And even as he told them that this could go nowhere, they countered with how much they liked him. No, no, they insisted, they *really* liked him. For *himself.* It had nothing to do with him being royal—they just liked him *incredibly* much…

He was bored with their fawning, and he knew that he was arrogant and not that nice—he knew there was nothing in him to like aside from his title.

He looked over to Antonietta, who gave an appreciative eye-roll that said her pasta was truly divine.

It was refreshing to sit in silence. To *want* to know more about someone else. And so it was Rafe who spoke. 'What made you change your mind?'

'I never got to make up my mind,' Antonietta said. 'He was the golden boy of the village.'

'Was?'

'He has married and moved away now, but

at the time he was the star of Silibri—funny, charming, a hard worker. Everybody loves Sylvester. My father thought he was choosing well…'

'But?'

Antonietta did not know how to answer that. She did not know how to tell Rafe that Sylvester's kisses had left her cold, and that his hands had felt too rough. And that she'd had a sense of fear that had pitched in her stomach whenever she was alone with the man who had been chosen for her.

It wasn't loyalty to Sylvester that halted her, and nor was it Antonietta's propensity never to gossip. Instead it was a new layer of confusion that Rafe had inadvertently added to the mix—for she wanted *his* hand to close again around hers.

They were mid-meal, of course, but his earlier touch had bemused Antonietta, for not only had she liked it, it had felt like the most natural thing in the world. And touch had never come naturally to her.

'Have you seen him since?' Rafe asked when she refused to elaborate on what it was about Sylvester that had caused her to change her mind.

'No. When I got to Paris I wrote and apologised. He never responded and I don't blame him for that.'

'What about your parents?'

'They have had nothing to do with me since. I understand, though. I didn't just shame them. I embarrassed the whole family on both sides…'

'That's surely to be expected when the bride and groom are related?'

'Don't!' She gave a shocked laugh, but then it faded. 'I'm coming to realise that they're never going to forgive me.'

'The question is, can you forgive *them*?'

'Forgive *them*?'

'Antonietta, I'm sure you had your reasons for running away.'

She didn't answer with words. Instead it was Antonietta's skin that spoke, as a blush spread across her chest and cheeks.

'Quite sure,' Rafe said.

'They weren't to know,' she responded, in hot defence of her parents, but Rafe remained unmoved.

'I have known you for only a few days,' he said. 'And I *know* that you had your reasons. I don't know what they were, but I am certain they exist.'

Antonietta swallowed and then reached for her wine, took a gulp and swallowed again.

'You can tell me,' he offered.

'Why would I?' Antonietta retorted. 'You leave tomorrow.'

'That makes me the perfect sounding board,' said Rafe, refusing to match her sudden anger. 'You never have to see me again.'

It was, she silently conceded, oddly appealing.

'However, if you don't want to speak about yourself any more you can ask about me,' he invited. 'Or perhaps you already know?'

'I don't know anything about you,' Antonietta admitted. 'Some of the staff have tried to tell me, but I close my ears to gossip and I never pry.'

'Pry away,' Rafe said, for although he had done his best to maintain their privacy, there was a chance she would wake up to the tabloids telling her she had dined with a playboy prince.

'You'll answer anything?' Antonietta checked.

'Not necessarily.' He would tell her his title, Rafe had decided. Generally, that more than sufficed.

Yet the question she had for Rafe was not about that. 'Where did you get those bruises?'

His eyebrows rose in surprise at her question. 'Skiing,' he said.

'An accident?'

'Not really. It was more recklessness on my part.'

'Oh. So you're here in Silibri to recover?'

'I'm here to lie low for a while,' Rafe said.

'And you're *not* married?'

'I've already told you, no.'

'Or involved with anyone?'

Rafe's jaw gritted a fraction. Couldn't she just ask the simple question and be done? Once she knew he was the Crown Prince of Tulano this attempt at a get-to-know-you would end.

For no one really knew the Crown Prince.

'I'm not serious about anyone.'

'Have you ever been?'

'Why all these questions?'

'You told me I was free to pry!'

So he had. 'No,' Rafe said. 'I have never been serious about anyone.' He thought back. 'I tried to be once,' he said. He glanced up and saw that she sat still and silent. Patiently waiting. 'Or rather, I tried to make things work. But I was barely in my twenties.' He looked into her sad treacle-black eyes and appreciated her lack of comment. 'I disappointed a lot of people when we broke up. Though I guess you would know all about that?'

'Were you engaged?'

'God, no!' Rafe said. 'If that had been the case there would have been no going back.'

The way he said it made her shiver. That dark note to his tone struck a warning that she had no idea of the power she was dealing with.

As delectable as her pasta was, Antonietta put her silverware down, and as the waiter removed her plate she braced herself to ask the final question.

But when push came to shove she found that she dared not. 'Rafe, on a couple of occasions I have tried to find out who you are. But the truth is I am a little nervous to know.'

'Why?'

'Because…' She flailed around for an explanation. 'Because I don't want to feel any more daunted than I already do.'

'You feel daunted?'

'A bit,' she admitted. 'A lot.'

'I don't want you to feel daunted,' Rafe said, and again he took her hand.

'Which is why I don't want to find out that you're a film star, or a world champion skier…'

She floundered in her poor attempts to label him, for she was certain he was rather more than that. She knew it from the way he held himself, and the silent command of his presence. She knew that heads had turned as they entered the restaurant, and they had not, despite his kind words, turned for her.

She looked down at their entwined fingers. Oh, it was not just his hands that gave him away, but they had hinted at the truth from the start. Yes, there really were only two reasons that men had manicures: they chose to or they were born to.

She did not want to know.

'So you think I could be a film star or a world

champion skier?' Rafe teased. 'Absolutely not, to the former, and I wish, to the latter.'

And then it was Rafe who had a question, and he both frowned and smiled when he asked it.

'Why wouldn't you want me to be a champion skier?'

She blushed instead of answering.

'Why?' Rafe asked again.

'I would like to see the dessert menu,' Antonietta said, and sidestepped the question.

Rafe left it.

For now.

'I can't decide!' Antonietta groaned as she read through the menu, because everything sounded sublime.

'When there is Modica chocolate mousse on the menu,' Rafe said, with barely a glance at the other offerings, 'the choice is already made.'

He gave her a quizzical look as she started.

'What?'

'Nothing,' Antonietta said, thinking of the purchase she had made that morning with Rafe in mind. It would be foolish to tell him, surely? But then she looked into the eyes of the man who had been so very kind to her today and it made it a little easier to reveal. 'I bought some for you.'

'For *me*?'

Antonietta nodded. 'For Christmas. Well, that was when I thought you were staying until Christmas Eve.'

In Silibri, gifts were often exchanged then. Though it wasn't often that a chambermaid bought a gift for a guest, and they both knew it.

She opened her mouth to say that she had bought it because he had been kind when she cried. But of course that would be a lie, for she had bought it before that had happened.

'It's just a small thing,' she settled for instead. 'A tiny little thing.'

Yet it touched Rafe.

'Coffee-flavoured,' Antonietta said.

'With a breakfast banquet at the side?' he checked, taking them both back to the morning they had met.

'No!' Antonietta smiled.

'You were the only good thing that happened that day.'

'I didn't do anything,' she pointed out.

'Antonietta, I find your silence golden.'

Their desserts arrived, and with them a silver platter which, the waiter told them, held real snow from the Nebrodi range. Nestled in it were two tiny glasses of icy Limoncello.

'Is this really snow?' Antonietta asked, pressing into it with her fingers.

'Apparently so,' Rafe said, pushing his own fingers in and finding hers. '*Not* what I need after a skiing accident. It's lucky it's not triggering a flashback.'

He made her laugh.

And to see her laugh felt like a reward.

The mousse was perfect and the Limoncello, though icy, was warming and a delectable end to their meal. Though the night did not have to end, suggested Rafe. Because they could dance.

'I told you, I don't dance,' she attempted to say. But when he ignored her and stood up, held out his hand, she decided that Aurora was right and this dress did deserve at least one dance.

Or two. For how could he be so tall and so broad and yet so graceful? Antonietta wondered as she melted in his arms.

He carried her through it—not physically, but

through her missteps and clumsy efforts. And he only winced once.

'Did I step on your feet?' She gave a worried frown.

'No,' Rafe told her, and he said no more—just held her until she knew how to dance…but only with him.

He felt the tension slide out of her during the second dance, and he knew certain triumph as she relaxed in his arms. Somehow he knew this was rare for her. And he could not remember enjoying a night so much.

A night that could be considered tame by his usual standards, but by royal standards was both reckless and wild. Because she hadn't been palace-approved, as a true date would be, and neither had she signed disclaimers, as his usual companions would.

It was uncharted waters for both of them.

The music slowed further, as if the band had heard his silent request, and now he moved her closer.

Antonietta made no protest, for she wanted more contact and she liked the shield of his arms. The heat from his palm was in the middle of her back and his other hand was on her bare arm. He did not put a finger wrong.

Not one.

Yet her bare arm wished that he would.

She could feel the slight pressure of his fingers and she ached to know their caress. She wished the hand on her back would go lower, so much so that she suddenly found she was holding her breath.

'Antonietta?'

His head had lowered and his mouth was near her ear. His voice, so close, made her shiver.

'Yes?' she said, though she did not lift her face to him. Instead she opened her eyes to the fabric of his suit.

'Why don't you want me to be a world champion skier?'

She didn't answer straight away, and instead swayed to the beat as every exposed piece of flesh—and those hidden away beneath the red silk—burned in his arms.

'Because…' she started.

'I can't hear you.'

Now she lifted her head, and she had to

stretch her neck so that her red-painted lips were close to his ear.

'Aren't sportsmen supposed to be insatiable?'

'I don't know,' Rafe said. 'I have never been with one.'

She laughed, but then she was serious. 'I won't sleep with you,' she said again.

It was stated as fact, yet she knew it was a lie, because she was on fire in his arms and she was weak with want.

'Can I ask why?' Rafe said, for he could feel her desire.

She could have told him that she was scared to, or that she did not know how, and both of those answers would have been true, but there was another reason that was holding her back, and Antonietta voiced it now.

'Because I have a feeling that you would pay me.'

'I would pay for your discretion,' Rafe responded calmly. 'Not for the act.'

She pulled back and looked up into his eyes. 'I don't understand…'

'You would have to sign an NDA.' He registered her frown. 'A non-disclosure agreement.'

'That's the most unromantic thing I have ever heard.' She actually laughed.

'Tell me about it,' Rafe said. 'It is very inconvenient at times.'

How was she *laughing* at such a subject?

Why was she imagining them tumbling into bed and Rafe whipping out a contract for her to sign?

'It is just as well,' Rafe continued, 'that I am the least romantic man.'

Except he didn't seem unromantic to her. She had never felt more looked after, or been held with such care and skill, and she had never looked so deeply into a man's eyes while sharing a smile.

'But you can carry on dancing with me,' Rafe said, 'without signing a thing.'

He pulled her in so close that she could feel all she would be missing pressing into the softness of her stomach. His other hand was on her shoulder, toying with the spaghetti strap of her dress and making her breasts ache and crave for the same attention.

'Can you kiss me?' Antonietta asked, and her

voice was husky and unfamiliar. 'Without me having to sign a thing?'

'Of course,' he said, in a voice that was completely steady. 'But later.'

Kiss me now, she wanted to plead as his hand moved down to the small of her back and pressed her in a little more.

He smoothed the hair from her hot face and then slid his hand under the dark curtain and stroked her neck and the top of her spine. They hadn't even kissed, yet she was weak and breathless in his arms, and just when she thought she might die from wanting him he released her a touch.

'Why don't I take you home?' Rafe suggested.

He made her wait for her kiss.

Through handshakes with the owner and then out to the delicately lit street.

Now, she kept thinking. *Let it be now.*

But, no.

He took her hand and held it tightly as they walked to the car.

Now, please now, she thought, with the moon high in the sky as they drove through the hillsides.

But of course it would not be now, for she did not want the audience of his driver for their first kiss, even if there was a partition.

Rafe sensed that. He had done far more than kiss in the back of a luxury car, but he wanted this to be right.

He still held her hand, carefully moving it to his thigh, but that was all. And then he loosened his grip and left it there.

She felt the solid muscle beneath her hand and of course she was too shy to move her hand higher. But there was actually no need, for to rest her hand on his thigh was bliss enough.

And then the girl with the saddest eyes spoke and made her first joke to him. 'Champion skiers have very powerful thighs.'

He smiled. 'Perhaps I missed my vocation.'

He made her wait even longer as they arrived at her little stone cottage at the end of a perfect date, and he made one thing very clear.

'Don't ask me to come in, for I might find it impossible to leave.'

'I won't.' Antonietta nodded. She would not lower herself to deal with 'paperwork', but she did have one request. 'Can you ask your minders to leave, though?'

She was not just quiet, Rafe realised, she was shy, for the cars were all parked well away. He was about to point that out, and even possibly to add that they could not be less interested in a mere kiss, for they had seen far more. In truth, should he be asked in, they were the men who would speak with her first and get her signature on a page.

Except it was not a *mere* kiss.

And he would not be asked in.

'One moment.'

Dismissing Royal Protection Officers was not that easy, for though they were minding *him*, they answered to the King. And this was irregular indeed.

But in the end Rafe was Crown Prince, and when the Crown Prince told you, in no uncertain terms, to back the hell off because you were dismissed for the night, then—albeit reluctantly—you left.

She heard the crunch of gravel as the cars drove away and watched as Rafe walked back towards her—alone. She was nervous, but no longer daunted. He took her little purse from her hands and he took off her shawl. But it wasn't the night air that made her shiver as he placed them on the stone wall, it was the thought of the kiss to come.

He looked right at her as his fingers went to the spaghetti strap of her dress. They made a new language, one without words, for as his fingers toyed with the strap his eyes told her that he had wanted to do this on the dance floor. She swallowed as he pulled the strap down her arm, and she was shaking like a trapped bird as he lowered his head and kissed the bare skin.

Oh, his mouth was warm and soft, and then not so soft, more thorough and deep, and her lips parted, and her knees did not know how to keep her standing up.

No matter, for his hand slid around her waist and his mouth worked up her neck and then came to her mouth.

'All night,' Rafe said, 'I have wanted to kiss you.'

Antonietta had dreaded Sylvester's kiss, let alone the thought of anything more. She had never envisaged that she might ache for a man's kiss. But now, with her neck damp from his mouth and his hands on her cheeks, she was wound tight with anticipation, and desperate to know the weight of his lips on hers.

It was a soft weight, and at first it satisfied. The graze of his lips had her own mouth pouting to reciprocate and her eyes simultaneously closing. He kissed her slowly until she returned it, and when her lips parted she shivered at her first taste of his tongue.

She had never imagined that a mouth could be so sublime, that his tongue could dance her to pleasure. His hands slipped from her face and moved down her bare arms, and Antonietta remained in his kiss, felt the pleasure building. He kissed her harder, and she felt as if she were nailed to the wooden door by his mouth, by the hands that were on her ribcage and the stroke of his thumb on her breast.

It had her weak and yet faintly desperate. Yes, desperate. For his kiss no longer satisfied. Instead it shot need into her veins. And the way his hand cupped her breast and lightly stroked her felt as if he was stroking her on the inside.

Rafe wanted her.

Badly.

But she had stated her case. So he removed his mouth and looked down at her, flushed and wanting and desirous.

'Go inside,' he told her.

Yet she remained.

For it felt as if the sky had parted and she had glimpsed behind it—as if everything she had been told and all that she had assumed was wrong.

Her body *worked.*

She wanted Rafe's kisses.

She craved Rafe's touch.

Sylvester's taunts had pierced her, embedded themselves so deeply, and yet she felt them lifting now.

Rafe did not daunt her.

If anything, she felt as if he had freed her.

This elusive man, who housed so many secrets, had set her body on fire.

Antonietta glimpsed all that she had avoided and all she had never truly known she was missing.

But would that change if he knew about her lack of experience?

Rafe was used to sophisticated women—something she doubted she could be. Would her innocence douse his desire? For he had made it clear he wanted no strings. And in that moment neither did she.

For the first time in her life Antonietta wanted to be intimate with a man. To taste his kiss again and to know the bliss denied to her until now.

This was so different—so new and so transforming.

And her choice entirely.

Her usual caution lay somewhere between the furthest star and the moon. She knew now how good a kiss should be, and only wanted more of the same.

And so she said what was in her heart.

'Take me to bed.'

CHAPTER SIX

RAFE DID *NOT* recall his minders.

Antonietta removed her high heels and they walked hand in hand across the moon-drenched grounds of the monastery on a clear Silibri night.

Where there had been years of turmoil and angst, now there was clarity and certainty. For there was no thought as to the outcome, or to tomorrow, just the bliss of now and this night.

'We can't go through the foyer,' Antonietta said.

'Of course not,' Rafe agreed. 'I have my own entrance. Though you would…'

His voice trailed off and she felt his grip tighten on her hand. She looked up to see what had stopped him from speaking, though his stride did not falter.

Antonietta looked to where his gaze fell and there at the foot of the steps was a suited man—one of his security detail. She attempted a small joke. 'He can't stop you from entering, surely…?'

And then it was her voice that trailed off as she realised that of course it was not *Rafe* who was the problem.

It was her.

But the security man said nothing. He merely stepped aside. And as Antonietta glanced up at Rafe she saw why—the man would surely not dare to question him, for the look Rafe gave him could freeze molten lava and halt a lion's approach.

'Is there a problem?' Antonietta asked, recalling their conversation about 'paperwork'.

'Of course not,' Rafe said, for he knew he would deal with the issues raised tomorrow. And there would be issues—of that he was certain. For Antonietta had been neither vetted nor approved. And the security guard had unnerved her.

Rafe could not know of her trepidation as he pushed open the French windows and they stepped into the lounge of his suite.

The turn-down service had been in and a fire was lit.

'Would you like a drink?' he offered.

She was about to decline, but then she glanced at the open doors to the bedroom and saw the vast bed. She decided she needed to pause things for a moment, if only to slow her heartbeat down.

'Please.'

She took in a deep breath as he poured, and could not decipher whether it was terror or desire that coursed through her.

Both, she decided as they clinked glasses.

But a drink didn't hold him back for long.

'Come here,' he told her, and put down his glass.

Antonietta did the same, and as she walked towards him it felt less seamless, and his kiss was different too.

It was thorough, it was hungry, and she felt her bravado fading.

She was tumbling with confusion, on an impossible see-saw as she kissed him back. Because he sent her skywards with his hands, with his mouth, with the way he held her against him.

He took her hand and guided it to where he was hard, and she felt as if the giddy high of the sky and then her nerves had her meeting the ground with a thud.

And she did not know how to reach the sky again.

And she could not fake her way through it.

'Rafe…' She had to tear her mouth from his, had to force her breathless throat to form words. 'I've never…'

Rafe did not care if she had never been into one-night stands.

He did not care if this was not something she often did.

But then he saw her pupils were dilated—and not just with desire. He recognised fear, and though he held her still, he froze absolutely.

'I've never slept with anyone before,' she said.

He dropped her.

Oh, she did not actually tumble to the ground, but she felt the see-saw crash down and she sank further without his touch.

'And you didn't think to tell me?'

'I was hoping you wouldn't notice.'

'Not notice! What the—?'

How the hell could she possibly think he might miss such a detail? But then his eyes narrowed in suspicion.

'Or were you hoping that I'd be too far gone to care?' he accused.

'I don't know what you mean.'

She really didn't.

He watched as she pulled up the straps on her dress, her pert nipples visible beneath the sheer fabric because their arousal remained. It was a fire that would not die, and had her words not halted him they would have been locked together now, with no thought to the consequences.

Rafe knew it.

Absolutely he knew it.

And it was an unfamiliar thing—for he always maintained a semblance of control and never forgot he was royal.

'I don't know what you mean,' Antonietta said again, her voice rising this time, and Rafe felt the anger recede, for she *really* didn't know. She wasn't trying to trap him, he realised. She was clueless, not ruthless.

'You should have told me.'

'Yes,' Antonietta agreed. 'But if I had I would be tucked up in bed alone now.'

'Do you know why?'

'Because you want someone experienced. You want—'

'Antonietta,' he interrupted, 'I leave tomorrow.'

She didn't blink, he noted. At least not until a log on the fire dropped, and it spat sparks and hissed for a moment before it settled.

'I know that,' she said finally.

'If you have waited this long—'

'Oh, please don't!' Antonietta interrupted him now, a little embarrassed and a lot angry. 'Please don't tell me that I must be saving myself for marriage, for Mr Right…'

'Why have you waited, then?'

'Because.'

Now she was embarrassed, and she reached for her shawl rather than answer him. She picked up her bag, ready to head out into the night, but he caught her arm.

'Because?' he demanded.

'I've never wanted anyone until now!' She shouted it, and continued to shout. 'My fiancé kept trying and I loathed it. I loathed every touch and every kiss and every attempt—' Her chest shuddered as she took in ragged gulps of air.

'Every *attempt*?' Rafe checked. 'What do you mean?'

'He tried—several times—but I fought him off.'

There—she had said it and the sky had not fallen. She had told someone. In fact she had admitted to this man whom she had known only a few days, something she had never revealed to her family or even her dearest friend.

Perhaps it was because she knew Rafe was leaving, she pondered briefly.

'I told *him* that I was saving myself for marriage; it was the only way I could keep him back. So please don't assume you know my reasons for waiting.'

'Did he hurt you?' Rafe was aware of the anger in his own voice and fought to check it, for his anger was not aimed at her. Then he answered his own question. 'Of course he did.'

'No,' she countered. 'Not really.' For even all these years later there was no neat category for what had taken place on those long-ago nights, and she didn't want to discuss it. 'You are not a counsellor—and I came here to move on, not to look back.'

She looked down to his hand, still closed around her wrist, but looser now.

'I'll say goodnight,' she said.

Yet Rafe could not leave things there. He let go of her wrist, and as he watched Antonietta gather her things there were two people that Rafe loathed right now.

The man who had attempted to force her.

And the man who had tonight denied her.

'Antonietta…' He could see her confusion, could still feel the hum of angry words that hung in the air, and he did not want her leaving like this. 'I would never have brought you back here had I known you were a virgin.'

'We've already established that,' she clipped.

'Listen to me!' he snapped back.

And she liked it that he snapped. She liked his impatience, and the fact that he did not suddenly treat her like fragile glass, that her past did not change them.

'I am trying to explain…'

'You don't want me,' Antonietta said. 'I think you have made that exceptionally clear.'

'Of *course* I want you!'

He sounded cross, and yet his tone did not trouble her.

It felt like a row. Yet it did not unnerve her.

For when she looked, when she met his navy eyes, there was desire rather than ire blazing in his eyes.

And it almost floored her.

'Antonietta.'

He took a breath and it seemed to her as if he was preparing her for bad news.

'I *will* be leaving tomorrow.'

Was that it? The bad news? She knew that already.

'Rafe…'

She did not know how best to put it that she was not terrified of his leaving. She was terrified of being sent away!

Tomorrow? She had dreaded so many tomorrows. And she had loathed so many yesterdays.

'I don't care what happens in the morning.'

It sounded reckless, yet right now she felt no caution.

Rafe knew more about her than any other person on this earth. He knew her secrets. And with his kiss he had disproved her own theory, for it turned out that Antonietta *could* want, could be folded over with desire and crave a man's touch.

'I don't care that you're leaving tomorrow,' she told him. 'I care only that you're asking me to leave *now*.'

He weighed her words as he stood there. And they were heavy ones, for she was trusting herself to him.

'I'm not asking you to leave,' Rafe said. 'I'm just asking if you are sure.'

She was.

Absolutely.

As certain as she had been at the door to her cottage.

More certain than she had been as they'd walked on the moon-drenched grass.

Completely certain now.

And nervous.

Yet excited as Rafe took her hand and led her to the master bedroom.

* * *

It was warm in there. The turn-down service had been in and the fire was roaring. She wondered if he would open the French windows to let in some cool air, but instead he threw two more logs on the roaring fire and then came over to her.

'What am I to do with you?' Rafe asked, and she did not know how to answer. He smoothed back the hair from her face and his gaze was assessing. 'Are you scared?'

'No,' Antonietta said. 'Well, a bit—but not like I once was.'

The room was too hot, and they stood just a little too close to the fire. But she liked it. For the fire felt like an iceberg and the air seemed cool compared to the heat pooling low in her belly and spreading down her thighs.

Yet Rafe touched her not.

Deliberately so.

This would be no *attempt*.

He loathed it that she had been touched while unwilling, and he would not move even so much as a finger until she approached him, though he'd offer direction.

'Take off your dress,' he told her, and she blinked, because she had thought that Rafe would take care of that. But Rafe did not cajole her, he did not sweet talk or wheedle, he simply made her want.

And it felt delicious.

For the first time ever she rued Aurora's dressmaking skills, for it took her a moment to find the tiny concealed zip at the side. She pulled it down with shaky hands and then stood trembling and a little shy as it fell to the ground.

She stood only in her knickers. As a reflex, she covered her breasts with her arm. But then she pondered her own disappointment if Rafe were to undress and do the same, and she took a breath and peeled her arm away, let it fall to the side.

Rafe cast his gaze the length of her slender frame, to her pert breasts and the dark areolae, the stiffened nipples that he ached to touch—but resistance was a turn-on, he was finding.

She pushed her knickers down without his instruction, and had to put a hand up, resting it on his chest to steady herself. He hissed out a long intake of breath.

He reached out and traced one manicured finger from her collarbone to her breast, until her own breath choked her. The feel of his hand on her breast was sublime and she looked down, somewhat fascinated. For the room felt like a sauna, and yet her dark nipples peaked to his touch as if they were smeared in Nebrodi snow.

He was sure that she was sure.

So sure that he lifted her by the hips and their mouths met as if deprived. She coiled her legs around his torso and his hand roamed her naked body as they kissed.

She did not know how sexy she was, Rafe thought, for he had thought her shy and reticent and yet she came alive in his hands.

He wanted to tear off his clothes, just to feel her naked against him, but there was a supreme pleasure in her naked warm body wrapped around him.

He placed her down on the bed that she had made that very morning. The sheets that smelt of summer were cool and yet soft on her naked skin, and she made no attempt to cover herself, just lay and watched as he undressed.

She had seen him nearly naked, but on those

occasions she had averted her eyes and tried not to look. Now there was no need to be chaste, or embarrassed by her inquisitiveness, and she watched unashamedly as he peeled off his shirt and revealed his chest.

Rafe was impatient to be naked and to join her. Rarely did he have to tell himself to slow down, and yet her hungry eyes beckoned. The rosy blush spread as if she held a fan across her chest and cheeks, and the way she bit down on her lip as he unbuckled his belt made undressing a less than seamless task, for he could not tear his eyes from her.

Nor could she tear hers from him. For she might have seen him *nearly* naked and considered him perfection, but completely exposed Rafe was magnificent.

Far more magnificent than she knew what to do with.

And when she saw him, so strong and erect, there was a stroke of desire so low in her stomach that she pulled up her knees.

'Don't be scared,' he told her.

'I'm not,' Antonietta said, in a voice that sounded too thick and too low.

And then she looked at him again, and wondered how they might possibly fit.

But she was *not* scared. She knew that because before fear had made her fight like a cat and slam her legs closed.

Fear had never made her approach. And it was not fear that had her rising to her knees and prowling across the bed towards him.

For the first time they were face to face, and yet only for a moment did they look into each other's eyes. There was so much to explore, to touch and to feel, and Antonietta had been resisting doing so almost since they had met, since their first conversation.

But now she could touch those wide shoulders, feel their strength and his warm skin beneath her fingers. Now she could run her hand down his chest and explore the mahogany nipples, pressing the pads of her fingers in. She ached to kiss them, and yet there was even more she ached to feel. She perused the taut planes of his stomach and then turned her hand so the backs of her fingers brushed the snaky line of dark hair.

Daring herself, she touched his thick member, surprised when it twitched as she held him alive and firm in her nervous palm. He slid through her hands and Rafe let her explore him, though his teeth were gritted together, for he longed to wrap his hand tight over hers. But to show her his rhythm would finish him, so he sank into her untutored perusal and explored her instead.

His hands were light on her breasts, yet her nipples hardened further and almost stung, so that she yearned for the wetness of his mouth. He did not give it. Instead his hands slid slowly down, past the curve of her waist, and held her hips, pulling her closer to him and rocking her, so that he nudged against her and left a silver trail on her stomach.

Her breathing hitched and she did not know how to get it back to its rhythm. When his hand slid between her thighs she gave in, and just rested her head on his chest.

Her soft moans spoke of her pleasure as he parted damp curls. Feeling her warm and ready, Rafe slid his fingers into her warm folds and explored her.

'There…' she breathed.

It was a needless instruction, because he already was there, but she pressed her face into his chest and inhaled his scent. One large hand cupped her buttock as the other burrowed into her tight, warm space.

And she didn't just let him—Antonietta *wanted* him.

She wanted the tiny volts of pleasure he shot through her, and she wanted the salty taste of his skin on her lips and tongue, and the tears that squeezed from her eyes were absolutely ones of pleasure.

And when he was sure she was ready—when he could feel she was on the delicious edge, and when he knew that her pleasure might finish him—Rafe withdrew his hand and opened the bedside drawer.

The tearing of foil felt like a zip tightening low in her stomach, and Antonietta watched, held in a spell of his making, as he sheathed himself.

She bit down on her lip rather than admit that she preferred the velvet skin naked.

But then her lip broke free, and unwittingly

she voiced her thoughts. 'I want to feel you in me…'

Rafe pulled a breath in. Those words from anyone else would have served as a warning. Yet tonight those words were a mirror of his own thoughts.

'And you shall,' he told her as he laid her down.

The room was almost stifling, yet it only heightened the pleasure. Her body was flushed and pliant, and when he came over her Antonietta's mouth met his.

He nudged at her entrance and she closed her eyes as he finally took her—took her there and back on a spectrum of pleasure and pain as he filled her.

Her hands gripped his shoulders and he gritted his teeth. 'Your shoulder…' she gasped.

She knew then what his grimace on the dance floor had been about, but as she went to remove her hands his pain was forgotten, and she dug her fingers further in as he filled her so absolutely that it felt there wasn't even enough space to gather in a necessary deep breath.

Instead, she held on to her breath and to a scream.

She had been right. They did not fit.

Yet for Rafe the tight grip of her was so intense that he let out a moan as he fought to stay still while she grew accustomed to the feel of him inside.

She would never accustom herself, Antonietta was sure. Except now his ragged breathing in her ear was coming into focus, and her grip was loosening on his shoulder, and she was so warm she felt she might faint.

'I want a drink of water,' she said, and heard his low laughter in her ear.

He gave her his mouth and he kissed her softly, so that she forgot the agony she was in. More velvet-soft kisses and then he moved deep inside her until she could no longer focus on his kiss.

She slumped back on the bed and he slid an arm under her, and when he moved she did the same.

'Rafe…' She said his name and he tempered himself, fought to slow down, but that was not what she was asking. 'More…'

She had never known anything so delicious—until he put his elbows to the sides of her head and looked right down into her eyes, sweeping damp hair from her face. Then Rafe started to thrust, and she held not his chest, nor his shoulders. She stroked her fingers down his back and felt his taut buttocks, pressed him harder into her.

How did he know? she wondered, because she'd closed her eyes and told him nothing, but he was thrusting harder now.

'Rafe…' she said again, but there was no instruction she could give when he was playing her like a master.

He felt the shivers of her orgasm even before Antonietta knew what was happening.

He was moving faster, and she could see the concentration on his features. The tension seemed to rip through her, and she clenched tight, but he thrust harder.

Rafe came in blessed relief, and her deep pulses dragging him in were his reward. And then his breathless moan reverberated through her as she convulsed beneath him. He felt her soft collapse as her body relaxed.

'I never knew…' Antonietta was breathless as he lay atop her, dragging in air. 'All I was missing…'

'Because you never knew *me*.'

CHAPTER SEVEN

JUST AS SHE always was, Antonietta was up long before the Sicilian winter sun. And for a moment she languished in bliss. Her head lay on Rafe's chest and she listened to the *thud, thud, thud* of his heart, and in the silence of predawn she focussed only on the sheer pleasure of waking next to him.

The hurt that had become so familiar was held at bay when she was in his arms, and it was incredibly tempting to sink back into the sleep that beckoned. She fought it, though. The consequences of being caught in a guest's bed had started to impinge and Antonietta forced her eyes open.

'Rafe…' She tried to untangle herself from the heavy arm that lay over her. 'I had better head back to the cottage.'

'Not yet,' he said sleepily.

'Yes,' she insisted. 'Your coffee will be delivered soon, and I had better not be here! I ought to leave while it's still dark.'

'I'll walk you back.'

It was an offer without precedent, for while Rafe always ensured that his dates were seen home, it was generally under the care of his driver. Not that Antonietta could know that.

Even so, she immediately shook her head. 'No, the staff will soon be starting to arrive,' she said as she hauled herself from the warm bed and pulled the drapes open enough to allow her to see and scramble for her clothes. 'I cannot be seen leaving your room.'

It really was unthinkable.

Most certainly she would lose her job. And, worse, her reputation in the village—already shaky at best—would flatline completely.

Last night it had felt so simple and straightforward, but the encroaching light of dawn cast shadows of doubt.

Rafe had promised one night, which meant their time was over, but how could this be goodbye? How did she simply walk out of his life as if their parting did not matter to her?

Because it did.

It very much did.

Rafe turned on the bedside light and Antonietta hurried to finish dressing. She turned her back to him, though not because she was suddenly shy—she was trying to hide her eyes. She did not want Rafe to glimpse, even for a second, that last night's bravado had gone.

'Tomorrow' was here.

Which meant he was leaving today.

Antonietta couldn't say that she hadn't been warned. The potential for hurt had been clearly labelled, just as a pharmacist added stickers to a medicine bottle.

May cause heartbreak.

In case of sudden tears do not attempt conversation.

And so Antonietta did up the tiny zip on her dress, pulled on her shoes, and then turned to Rafe and attempted a smile. 'Thank you for a wonderful night.'

He lay with his hands behind his head, watching her dress and wanting to haul her back into bed. Sex had made him hungry, and he would love nothing more than to confuse the chefs and cancel his strict order for coffee only, then tear into pastries and make love to her all over again.

'Stay a little longer. I'll order breakfast.'

'I'm not hiding in the bathroom, Rafe. Anyway, I really do have to go to work.'

She did not want prolonged goodbyes and to be told by him that it had been good while it lasted.

Make that *great.*

Or rather, make that the single best time of her entire life.

And it wasn't just the sex, though her body felt deliciously bruised and awoken. More, it had been the talking and the dancing, and walking across the Old Monastery grounds hand in hand.

And, even more than the sum of all that, it had been the honesty she had found with him. Even if it was impossible to be honest now, and admit that leaving with a smile was the hardest thing she had ever done.

Absolutely the hardest.

She went over and gave him a kiss.

A light one was her intention—except Rafe moved his hand behind her head and pressed her close. Antonietta closed her eyes to the taste and the bliss. She was tempted, so tempted to give in. Was he subtly guiding her to lie atop him, or was she actually drifting that way to the command of his kiss?

Their tongues were more urgent, the kiss deeper as his other hand moved to her breast, toying with it through the fabric of her dress, and Antonietta knew he would have far less trouble with the zip than she.

Rafe's moves were seamless, and Antonietta knew that any moment she would be naked and knotted with him, locked into bliss with no thought as to the ramifications there would surely be.

And she would fall deeper.

Self-preservation had Antonietta removing her mouth, and she looked down for a moment into his deep navy eyes and knew she could very easily drown in them.

Do not take more than the stated dose...

Or she might never recover.

'Be good,' she said.

He gave a slight mirthless laugh. 'I don't want

to be good.' But then he was serious. 'You're okay?'

'Of course.'

'You're sure?' Rafe checked, and watched as her eyes narrowed a touch.

Would he prefer that she cried? Antonietta wondered. Well, she refused to allow him back into her thoughts. She had been a willing participant last night and did not regret it for a moment. It was just that she had missed the part in life's guidebook about how to walk from someone who mattered. The lesson that taught you how to be incredibly close one moment and say farewell the next.

'Goodbye, Rafe.'

Yes, walking through the French doors and climbing down the stone steps really was the hardest thing she had ever done.

Leaving a packed church full of people waiting for the bride to arrive had been a very public hurt. Being disowned by her parents had caused anguish and pain. But it was the price she had paid for rejecting Sylvester, and despite the consequences she knew she would do it again.

This was a private hurt that no one knew of.

The guard gave her a bored look as she passed, which told her that a woman leaving Rafe's bed was hardly noteworthy.

The birds were starting to sing and the sky was starting to lighten as she crossed the grounds, and the world carried on as if nothing had changed.

Yet for Antonietta, everything had.

She looked back to the Old Monastery, and more specifically to the August Suite, from which she had just come. The master bedroom was in darkness, and she could almost picture Rafe reaching out and flicking the switch on the lamp before drifting off to sleep.

But Rafe had not gone back to sleep. Instead, he lay in the dark, in a bed perfumed by their union.

He had come to Silibri not just to lie low but to prepare himself for the enormity of what lay ahead, and all that awaited him when he returned to Tulano.

He had come to Silibri to clear his head.

Not to lose it to a maid with sad eyes.

* * *

Just this once Antonietta would have liked to do one of Chi-Chi's *slowly-slowly* acts. She was sore, and tender, and she wanted to dwell on last night and wallow a while. But then nothing would get done.

'I think it is mean of Nico to make us work on Christmas Day…' Chi-Chi huffed as she refilled the selection of toiletries in one of the regular suites.

It was stunning, of course, and looked out towards the valley, but it was nowhere near as luxurious as the August Suite.

In truth, Antonietta was happy to have been allocated to the suites well away from there. Her ears were on tenterhooks, waiting for the sound of a helicopter's approach that might signal his leaving.

'Of course some staff have to work,' said Antonietta, dragging her mind to their conversation as she dragged the vacuum cleaner from the doorway. 'Are the guests supposed to make their own beds and get their own food? What would be the point of people taking a Christmas Break?'

'Well, there could be a skeleton staff,' said Chi-Chi, as she needlessly rearranged the herbal teabags. 'That way some of the staff who have been here since the place opened could have the day off.'

'Tell Nico.' Antonietta shrugged.

'I intend to,' Chi-Chi said. 'In fact—'

Whatever Chi-Chi's grand plans were, Antonietta chose not to hear them and switched on the vacuum cleaner. She turned it to full suction and wished that drowning out her thoughts of Rafe was as easy as drowning out Chi-Chi's whining voice.

'Antonietta!'

She heard her name and then heard it again.

'Antonietta!'

'What?' she snapped, wondering what gripe Chi-Chi had this time that couldn't possibly wait—except it was Francesca who was calling her.

'Scusi,' Antonietta said and turned off the vacuum. 'I didn't see you there.'

'That's fine. I can see that *you* are busy…' Francesca shot a look at Chi-Chi, who was suddenly polishing a mirror. 'Signor Dupont has asked for his room to be serviced and he has requested you.'

'But I thought he was checking out?'

'Checking out?' Francesca frowned. 'Where did you hear that?'

'I'm not sure…' Antonietta attempted to cover her mistake. 'I thought you said he wouldn't last until Christmas Eve?'

'Well, that might be the case, but for now he is here—and, given that he has been in the August Suite for a week now, it requires a deep service, so I shall come with you.'

Oh, God! Please, no, Antonietta thought as they left Chi-Chi to it and collected linen before taking the elevator and heading along the cloisters.

What on earth was Rafe thinking, requesting *her*? She had visions of him lying naked on the bed as she and Francesca walked in, and was actually sweating as Francesca knocked and then opened the door.

It would seem Rafe had better manners than that, though.

'He's out,' Francesca said, after she'd made herself known but got no response.

Thank you, Antonietta breathed to herself.

'Let's get started,' Francesca said.

It felt odd, being back in the August Suite after last night. There on the table were the glasses that they had drunk from, but Francesca soon whipped them away.

'It looks as if he had company last night. Antonietta, why don't you get started in the master bedroom?'

From riches to rags.

Well, not quite. But she was no longer his lover and she was back to being his maid.

First she swept out the fire before which he had slowly undressed her. It felt as if it had been a dream. And then she rebuilt it, adding kindling under the logs and kneeling back for a moment. But there was no time to daydream, so she went to make up the bed.

As she pulled back the heavy cover she had lain beneath she saw the evidence of her lost virginity.

It had not all been a dream.

Quickly, and with her cheeks burning red, she bunched up the sheet. She was about to toss it to the floor when, glancing up, she saw Francesca standing in the doorway, watching her.

'You're a good worker, Antonietta.'

'Thank you.'

'It doesn't go unnoticed.'

Was it still the bloodied sheet that she held in her hand that made her blush, or was she hearing a warning behind Francesca's words? Had Rafe asking for her to service his suite set off an alarm? Or had they been seen driving off last night?

Surely Francesca didn't know?

'Let me help you,' Francesca said, and together they made the bed with fresh linen, chatting while they worked. 'After this we need to set up the Temple Suite.'

'Is there a guest arriving?' Antonietta frowned, because there had been no mention at handover.

'Nico is flying in to take lunch with Signor Dupont in the restaurant.'

'Oh.'

'Birds of feather.' Francesca gave a tight smile as she wrestled a pillow into its case.

'I'm sorry?'

'Oh, I know Nico is happily married now, but let us not whitewash his past and make him a saint. He was as much a playboy as Signor—'

'Francesca,' Antonietta interrupted, even though Francesca was her boss. 'You know I don't like to gossip. Aurora is my dearest friend and Nico is her husband. Gabe is my godson.'

'Of course.'

The silence between them was a bit strained after that.

With the bed made, Antonietta swept out the fire in the main lounge and then ticked that off the list. Because it was a deep service there was high dusting and ledges to be wiped, but finally it was all finished. And then, because Francesca seemed to be watching everything she did, Antonietta checked each and every candle, despite knowing they hadn't been lit.

It was possibly Antonietta's only regret from last night—not to have seen the August Suite bathed in candlelight.

'I think we are done,' Francesca said. 'Why don't you head off? I shall head down to greet Nico.'

'But we have the Temple Suite to prepare.'

'You're on a half-day,' Francesca pointed out, and then stopped speaking as the door opened and Rafe walked in.

He wore black jeans and a black jumper and his hair was dishevelled. From the sand he'd brought in, Antonietta guessed he had been walking on the beach.

'*Buongiorno*, Signor Dupont,' Francesca said. 'We have just finished.'

'*Buongiorno, signor,*' Antonietta added dutifully, although her voice was barely a croak.

Rafe didn't return their greetings and gave only the vaguest of nods as he walked past them with barely a glance.

She could have kissed him there and then for his arrogant ways, for surely this must put paid to any suspicions Francesca might have.

'Have a nice half-day and a good day off tomorrow,' Francesca said. 'Do you still have Christmas shopping to do?'

'No...' Antonietta said, but then remembered the lipstick. 'Yes—I still have Aurora's present to get, and I would like to get something for Pino.'

And she wanted to get something for Francesca too, Antonietta thought as she left the Old Monastery. Oh, and Vera in the laundry. And then there was Tony and Vincenzo…

She had come back to Silibri to be reunited with her family, and if that didn't work then her plan had been to leave and never look back. Yet, despite making no progress with her family, she was starting to make friends here. Real friends.

But still, it was going to be a very lonely Christmas. And for different reasons than those she had imagined when she had first arrived in Silibri. Christmas meant that Rafe would be gone, and she did not know how she would deal with that.

Nico's chopper was hovering as she crossed the grounds, and she watched as the pilot skilfully landed the beast. To her delight it was not just Nico who stepped out but Aurora too, and she was holding little Gabe!

Aurora looked stunning. She wore a kingfisher-blue dress with killer heels and her hair was a tumble of raven curls as she waved and ran towards her friend. Gabe was all black curls too, and huge black eyes, and Antonietta simply melted when he smiled as she held out her arms to him.

'See,' Aurora said as her son went so readily to Antonietta, 'he knows you.'

'He really does.' Antonietta beamed. 'I didn't think you were coming back until Christmas Eve?' she said.

'I wasn't intending to,' Aurora explained as Antonietta let them into the cottage, 'but Nico has a friend in residence over at the hotel. They are having lunch so I thought Gabe and I could come and see you. I'll join them for coffee afterwards and then we'll head over to my parents'.' She gave a dramatic eye-roll.

'How are they?'

'Still demanding that Nico gives my idle brother work. I have said no, but Nico has backed down. He's going to tell him this afternoon he's got him a role. God help us,' she muttered. 'He didn't even move the logs from Geo's house when there were those wildfires.' Geo was Nico's late father. 'Instead he left it to *me*.'

'That was a long time ago,' Antonietta pointed out.

'And he has grown fatter and lazier since.

Honestly, families are—' She stopped herself. 'Sorry. That was insensitive of me.'

'It's fine.'

'Has there been any progress?'

Antonietta gave a non-committal shrug. No, there had been no progress with her family—if anything, they seemed to be going backwards. But there had been progress in her life. She was making friends—real ones—and she was putting down roots too.

And as for Rafe…

That felt like progress too, because even if they could go nowhere he had taught her so much about herself.

'I've brought your Christmas present,' Aurora declared. 'I'll put it under your tree. No peeking…' she said, and then looked at the little lounge, which was pretty much exactly as she had left it some weeks ago. 'No tree!'

'There's only me here.'

'But you love Christmas! Here,' Aurora said, and handed her a parcel—only Antonietta had nothing to give her surprise guest in return.

'I did have yours…' Antonietta blushed. 'Then I borrowed it. I have to get another.'

'Well, hurry up.' Aurora smiled. 'It is only a few days till Christmas.' She looked over at her great friend and gave a quizzical frown. 'Since when do *you* wear red lipstick?'

'Who said I got you red lipstick?' Antonietta attempted, but Aurora knew her too well.

'You always do,' Aurora answered. 'Even when you were in France, and we were barely in touch, you sent the same present each year. So how come you borrowed it?'

'I just decided to give it a try.' Antonietta shrugged. 'You've been nagging me to wear make-up for years.'

'With no luck, though!' Aurora's shrewd eyes narrowed. 'What's going on?'

'Nothing,' Antonietta said, and set about filling the coffee pot, even though Aurora said she didn't want one.

'Just water for me. Antonietta…is everything okay? You seem on edge.'

'Of course.'

Antonietta knew she was holding back, but though she wanted to confide, in this case she felt she could not. Aurora might be her best friend, but her husband was Nico—the owner of the Old Monastery. He wouldn't appreciate a maid fraternising with a guest.

Still, she was saved from explaining her sudden need for lipstick by the sight of little Gabe, tottering around the table on unsteady legs.

'You didn't tell me he was almost walking!'

'Watch this,' Aurora said, and held out her arms to Gabe. 'Show Antonietta what you can do!'

Antonietta held her breath as Gabe turned from the table and took two tottering steps unaided, and then fell into his *mamma*'s arms.

'Oh, look at you!' Antonietta beamed and clapped her hands. 'He's adorable.'

'He is,' Aurora agreed. 'And he knows it. Though he's in for a big shock when his little sister comes along…'

It took a second for the news to sink in. 'You're expecting?'

'Yes! Although only you are allowed to know for now! We're thrilled,' she added. 'I know it means we'll have two under two, but we want them to be close…'

It was wonderful news. This time last year Aurora had been pregnant and practically homeless. Now she was deliriously happy and with *another* new baby on the way!

'I feel sick this time, though,' Aurora admitted.

'Then what are you doing in a helicopter?'

'Flying is fine—it is food that upsets me. That is why I decided not to join Nico for lunch. I don't think me vomiting in front of the Crown Prince of Tulano would go down too well.'

It was the second big piece of news in as many minutes—not that Aurora could know the effect her throwaway comment had had.

'Crown Prince…?'

The smile Antonietta had been wearing slipped from her face, and as her legs turned to water she reached for the couch and sat down. On some level she had always known, but on hearing Aurora confirm it Antonietta crumpled and buried her face in her hands.

'Whatever's wrong?' Aurora said. 'Antonietta, what did I say…?' She came and put her arm around her friend's shoulder. 'Tell me.'

'I can't.'

'Is it Rafe?' Aurora asked—because she had seen her friend pale when she had mentioned his title. When Antonietta neither confirmed nor denied it, Aurora pushed for more. 'Has he been causing problems for you?'

'Problems?' Antonietta frowned. 'No…no.'

'You don't have to put up with it just because you are staff…'

'No, Aurora.' Her friend was on the wrong track. 'The only problem is how much I like him.'

She felt the hand on her shoulder tense and wondered if she had been wise to say anything. But apart from being the boss's wife Aurora was also her best friend, and in truth she desperately needed her trusted advice.

'I *really* like him,' Antonietta admitted.

'You've never said that about anyone before.'

'I've never felt like this before. Rafe took me out for dinner last night and it was absolute bliss. I wore the red silk dress that you made for me and I knew *happiness*, Aurora. He was wonderful to me.'

She saw the doubt in her friend's eyes. The same doubt Antonietta had seen there when she'd insisted her family would forgive her.

'He really was…' she said.

'You're in over your head, Antonietta.'

'I know that,' Antonietta said. 'I already knew that even before I found out he was royal.'

'He has the most terrible reputation with women.' Aurora was both abrupt and upfront. 'Rafe makes Nico look tame, and I don't even know half of what Nico got up to before we were married.' She was genuinely concerned. 'Antonietta, don't let him use you.'

'*Used* was how I felt with Sylvester,' Antonietta admitted. 'I've never felt that way for a moment with Rafe.'

'Listen to me,' Aurora urged. 'Crown Prince Rafael is his father's son—everybody says so. You must have heard all the scandals attached to the King of Tulano?'

Antonietta had. Oh, they weren't sitting there at the forefront of her mind, but there were little memories of her mother tutting over a magazine. And there had been some scandalous articles she'd read laboriously when she'd been trying to improve her vocabulary in France.

'Rafe is exactly the same.'

'Rafe isn't married.'

'That doesn't give him free rein! He is irredeemable, Antonietta, and a complete rake. You must have looked him up?'

'No! I make up my own mind about people,' Antonietta said rather piously, and then stepped down from her high horse and admitted the truth. 'I've tried to look him up, but I can't get on the Internet here and I daren't risk it at work.'

'Well, don't bother—just heed my advice and stay well away from him,' Aurora warned, and then she looked at Antonietta's pale cheeks. 'Or am I right in guessing it's too late for that and he didn't just take you for dinner?'

Antonietta said nothing.

'Oh, Antonietta…'

It wasn't the best catch-up with her friend. Antonietta had wanted advice—only not the advice she had got.

And although Aurora wanted to be delighted for her friend, who had tucked herself away for far too long, she could not bring herself to it.

'I have to go over there now,' she said, picking up Gabe's little jacket. 'I'll try not to kill Rafe when I see him.'

'Please don't say anything,' Antonietta begged.

'Of course I won't.'

'Why don't you leave Gabe with me?' Antonietta offered. 'I can give him his birthday present…'

'You're sure?' Aurora checked. 'He's due for his afternoon sleep and it would be so much easier.'

'Of course I'm sure.'

'I'll leave my phone too,' Aurora said. 'It's got a good signal.'

Antonietta frowned, wondering for a moment why Aurora would leave her phone here when she was heading out, but then realised she was being given an opportunity to look Rafe up.

'That won't be necessary,' she said, but Aurora was blowing kisses to Gabe as she headed off for coffee with her husband and Rafe…

Rafe had found, during a long and luxurious lunch, that he'd had to keep pulling his focus back to the conversation with Nico. His mind had kept drifting to last night. Or rather it had kept honing in on *tonight*, and seeing Antonietta again.

All thoughts of checking out had gone and, knowing that she was on a half-day, he had decided that he would not wait until evening. If he walked Nico to his helicopter he could make a diversion to the cottage unnoticed…

'Ah, here is Aurora now,' Nico said, and both men stood as she approached the table.

As Rafe greeted her with the familiar kiss to the cheek, it was confirmed that she and Antonietta really were chalk and cheese. A person had to dig deep to get so much as a glimpse of Antonietta's thoughts, whereas Aurora wore her heart on her sleeve.

'Rafe,' she said as they greeted each other.

And, though it wasn't quite the Sicilian kiss of death, he could feel Aurora's wrath and suspicion even as they brushed cheeks, and was certain that she knew what had transpired last night.

'It is lovely to see you again,' Rafe said.

'Likewise.' Aurora gave a tight smile.

'Is Gabe with Antonietta?' Nico checked.

'Naturally,' Aurora said. 'Why wouldn't I leave him with my dearest friend? She *is* his godmother, after all.' She looked over to Rafe. 'I consider Antonietta family.'

'Of course...' Nico frowned, with no idea of what Aurora was alluding to.

Rafe knew, and he could feel Aurora's contempt when she addressed him.

'I was sorry to hear of your accident, though clearly you are feeling much better.'

'Much,' Rafe agreed. 'And I was just telling Nico how much I've enjoyed my stay here.'

'Any time,' Nico said. 'You are always welcome here, and I shall always do my best to ensure that your time in Silibri goes unreported. Consider the August Suite your bolthole.'

'I am sure,' Aurora said, 'that Rafe will soon grow bored with all Silibri has to offer.'

He could feel her animosity, and in truth it was merited. Rafe knew that he had earned his poor reputation with women. And he knew, too, that his time had run out and very soon he would have to settle down.

Nico's suggestion that he use Silibri as a bolt-hole had rattled Rafe—because it appealed. He sat making polite small talk with his hosts as visions of regular returns to Silibri scrolled in his mind.

And then he shocked himself by imagining how much nicer this gathering would be if Antonietta had joined them.

Rafe had always enjoyed Nico's company, although it had taken a new direction since his friend had settled down, and now took the form of tame lunches rather than parties aboard Rafe's yacht.

But to say there could be no future for himself and Antonietta was the understatement of the century.

Well, no tangible future, anyway.

She could be vetted, of course, and liaisons arranged beyond the reach of a camera lens. But Rafe knew even at this early stage that Antonietta deserved far more than that.

'We should get going,' Nico said now, but as farewells were exchanged, Aurora took another shot.

'So you will be going home for Christmas?' she checked. 'Or, given how well you have recovered, perhaps sooner?'

Rafe heard the veiled threat and was about to make a smart reply—for he did not appreciate being told what to do by anyone, let alone a newly married friend's wife. Except her concern was merited. And in truth he was grateful that Antonietta had Aurora on her side.

'There is a lot to take into consideration before I leave.' Rafe met her gaze, and with solemn eyes told her he had heard her concerns. 'Believe me, I am giving it much thought.'

So much thought that instead of strolling across the grounds to wave them off, and 'dropping in' on Antonietta, Rafe resisted the pull and headed back to his suite.

The thought of being with Antonietta appealed way more than it should. But he was a prince who needed no distractions, and it was time to pull back.

For Antonietta, the conclusion was the same.

She had spent an adorable hour playing with

Gabe and the little wooden train. He was an absolutely beautiful baby, with dark curls and big brown eyes, and just the distraction she needed for a confused and troubled heart.

Aurora's phone, resting on the table, had called to her, but Antonietta had resisted.

'Look,' she'd said, waving the train again. But after an hour it had become clear, even though Gabe took it, that all he wanted to do was sleep. Eventually Gabe had thrown the toy down, and Antonietta had only been able to smile, because he'd reminded her then of Aurora.

'You win,' Antonietta had said, pulling cushions from the sofa.

She'd made Gabe a little bed on the floor and in a matter of moments he'd been asleep.

By then Aurora's phone had developed its own magnetic pull, and she hadn't been able to help walking over to it.

You don't want to know, Antonietta had told herself.

Oh, but she did.

It hadn't taken her long to find out that Aurora's dark assessment of Rafe had been correct. Crown Prince Rafael of Tulano did indeed live a life of excess. There were endless photos, taken from a distance, but zoomed in enough, capturing the depravity taking place aboard his yacht. On land he was no better, be it *après ski* or falling out of casinos, and always, *always* with a beauty hanging off his arm.

Yet his lovers remained nameless and they *never* told all.

She'd been able to find no interviews, no bitter tears spilled in the glossies. He paid for their silence, Antonietta guessed, and finally she understood his reference to 'paperwork'.

His life of excess was not just with women. Antonietta had winced at the photos of a sports car wrapped around a tree, from which he had been cut out. And there had been falls from horses and an accident involving jet skis.

Yet through it all his people still adored him, despite seeming to wish for their Prince to slow down.

He showed few signs of doing so.

There were a couple of relationships she'd found, although they went way back. A Lady from England and a minor European royal it seemed he had dated for a while. Although on closer inspection she'd seen that it had been close to a decade ago. The press had gone wild with speculation both times, anticipating marriage, but those relationships had quietly faded and Crown Prince Rafael had reverted to his wild ways.

When Aurora had come to collect Gabe, it had been a shaken but resolute Antonietta who'd opened the door.

'We've got five minutes,' Aurora had said. 'Nico is just meeting with Francesca. How was Gabe?'

'Perfect,' Antonietta had said. 'He's sound asleep. How was your catch-up?'

'You mean how was Rafe?'

'No.' Antonietta had shaken her head firmly. 'I've decided you're right. I won't be seeing him again, even if he asks. And I won't—'

'Antonietta.' Aurora had interrupted her and plonked herself down on the floor beside her sleeping baby, playing with his little black curls. 'What if I'm wrong?'

'You're not wrong, though! I just looked him up and you gave me good advice.'

'Perhaps…' Aurora had sighed.

'Anyway, he's leaving.'

'He gave no indication that he was.' She'd looked up at Antonietta. 'Do you remember that night when the whole village was threatened by fire and you knew Nico was back and staying at my parents'…?'

'Of course.'

'Everyone had told me to get over Nico, yet you told me to go and fix what I could.'

'There was something there to fix, though. You and Nico had been promised to each other for ever…'

'Antonietta, the fact that you like Rafe speaks volumes to me. I don't *want* to like Rafe. I want to tell you to stay the hell away from him and I want to tell him the same, but…'

Then Aurora had taken a breath and told her friend something she never had before.

'When I was in Rome for staff training last year and I ran into Nico he wanted a one-night stand. Another one,' Aurora had added, and given a mirthless laugh. 'I denied him, of course. I refused to be used again. And I walked away. I was so proud of myself for resisting him, but by the next morning it had turned into the biggest regret of my life. I regretted it so much that I threw a coin in the Trevi Fountain and pleaded to have that time over again. And I got it!'

'There's no future for Rafe and me,' Antonietta had pointed out, and then she'd given a wry smile. 'And there's no Trevi Fountain here.'

'What I'm trying to say is that even if Nico and I had never come to anything I would not have regretted the time we spent together in Rome.' She'd looked over to Antonietta. 'You just have to—'

'I know what you're going to say,' Antonietta had interrupted. 'If I see him again I just have to hold on to my heart.'

'No.' Aurora had shaken her head. 'Do you trust him?'

Antonietta had thought for a moment.

Oh, there was a whole lot of evidence not to, but while her head told her to be cautious, her heart said otherwise. She thought of her time with Rafe. The man who had taught her to dance and so much more.

'Yes, I believe that I do.'

'Then you have to do the bravest thing and let go of your heart.'

CHAPTER EIGHT

BUT THERE WAS no opportunity to let go of her heart. No chance to proceed, even with caution, for there was no gentle knock at her door that night.

She slept fitfully and awoke with a jolt, unsure if she had missed the sound of Rafe's chopper leaving. It was her last day off before Christmas, and though Antonietta knew she should head into the village to finish her shopping, she couldn't face it.

This afternoon, perhaps, but right now she had never felt less Christmassy in her life.

She pulled on a denim skirt, a thin jumper and flat shoes and decided a walk might clear her head.

The temple ruins had been her and Aurora's playground. As little girls they would go there to play and lose an entire day, sitting on the steps and watching each other sing, or running through the columns. Aurora had loved the remains of the altar in the cellar area and would dress it with flowers and dream out loud about her wedding to Nico.

Aurora had always known what she wanted—family and home, Nico and babies, and all that she held dear on this very spot on earth…

But Antonietta had always looked beyond. Even as a little girl she had sat hugging her knees and looking out, dreaming of places, some near, some far. Picking up the orange dirt, she would run it through her hands and imagine grains of Saharan sand. There was a whole world she hadn't seen, and as Aurora sang, Antonietta would lie back on the stone and imagine that she lay in a glass igloo, looking up at the Northern Lights, or that she was stretched out on a manicured lawn at the Palace of Versailles…

She had tried that, Antonietta told herself now, and she had been told off for being on the grass.

Her ponderings were interrupted by the sight of Rafe, running in the distance. He was still here, then, and that brought a sense of relief in itself. His form was magnificent, his body a masterpiece, and she admired it for a stolen few moments before he noticed and ran in her direction.

'Hey,' she said as he approached. 'No minders?'

'I'm on the hotel grounds.'

'Not technically.'

She smiled, because the ruins were outside the boundaries of the Old Monastery. Then her smile slipped and she felt suddenly a bit awkward and shy. It had nothing to do with their lovemaking. Now she knew about his royal status, she couldn't pretend. It had been far easier not to know.

'I thought you were leaving yesterday?'

'That was the plan.'

'Why did you tell Francesca that you wanted me to service your suite?'

'I didn't,' Rafe said. 'I told her I did *not* want Chi-Chi.'

'Really?'

'Absolutely,' Rafe said.

He held out his hand and helped her to stand and they started walking. She offered him her water bottle and he took a long, refreshing drink.

'The ruins are spectacular,' Rafe said.

'I love them,' Antonietta agreed. 'Aurora and I used to play here when we were little. Or rather, Aurora used to play and I used to day-dream.'

'About what?'

'The world,' Antonietta said. 'This is where she and Nico were married.' She glanced side-ways at him. 'You weren't at their wedding?' She would certainly have remembered if he had been.

'No, I had prior engagements,' Rafe said.

And usually he would have left it at that. Cer-tainly, he rarely explained himself, and yet he found himself telling Antonietta more than he usually would.

'Nico and I are friends, yes, but perhaps not in the way you and Aurora are. It's more that we shared the same social scene for a while.'

'But not now?'

'No, not now. If that were the case I doubt Aurora would be pleased.'

'So, a bit wild?'

'Quite a bit.' He gave a wry laugh. 'You don't want to know.'

'But I do.' And then she was honest. 'I know who you are,' she admitted. 'Aurora told me.'

'And how does that make you feel?'

'Better and worse.'

Rafe frowned.

'Better because I understand now why this can go nowhere,' Antonietta said. 'And worse because I understand now why this can go nowhere.'

Rafe laughed ruefully and they carried on walking.

The air was cold on his cooling body and yet the company was invigorating. As they walked he told her something of his life. The endless calls to duty interspersed with a jet-set lifestyle, and the endless stream of heavily vetted company aboard luxurious yachts and invitation-only parties. And he told her how boring it got, for there was no fear of missing out when you were the draw card. And there was no thrill to the chase when all the women in the room had already signed a document to be discreetly yours.

But there were penalties to be paid for living in the fast lane, and he knew his reckless ways upset his people. 'I'm supposed to lie low until the bruises heal,' he said.

'They're still pretty spectacular,' she said, looking at his blackened shoulder and the purple lines there to match the yellow and grey ones she knew were on his ribs. 'And your eye is still black…'

Her voice trailed off because it could easily be covered with make-up, if he chose, since the swelling had all but gone now. Or she could paint him!

Antonietta gave a soft laugh as she recalled a time from her childhood.

'What's funny?' Rafe asked.

'I painted a rash on myself once. I was trying to get out of school.'

'Did it work?'

'I thought it did,' Antonietta said as they walked on in the crisp morning air. 'My *mamma* was worried and told me to stay in bed. I said I thought I might be strong enough to lie in the lounge and watch television.'

Rafe smiled.

'Then she said it was a very serious rash, and she would make me Sopa de Pat...' She glanced over and translated. 'Pig's feet soup. It is the thing I hate most in the world. But my *mamma* said it was the only cure for the rash I had.'

'And was it?' Rafe smiled.

'I did not wait to find out. I washed off the rash and told my *mamma* I felt better...'

And now she would be honest, which would take almost more courage than the other night.

'I would like to paint a rash on you, so you can stay a while.'

'I would like to stay a while too,' Rafe agreed. 'But it won't change the fact that I have to be home in time for Christmas. I am expected to join my family on the palace balcony on Christmas morning.' There was more to it than that, though. 'I've been rather reckless in my ways and those days are over.'

'Have you been told?' she asked.

'I have been told the same for more than a decade,' Rafe admitted, 'but I know that the time is now. I want to work hard for my country, and to do that I have to marry.'

'*Have* to?'

'I have been told that if I want more responsibility then I must tame my ways.'

This was not a conversation he had ever expected to have with a lover, for he always kept his distance, even in bed. Not with Antonietta, though, and Rafe tried, as gently as he could, to explain the future that had been dictated for him before he had even been born.

'I am to marry a bride my father and his advisors deem suitable. One who will further our country's connections and who understands the role of Crown Prince's consort.'

She asked him the same question he had asked her. 'And how does that make you feel?'

His answer was not so direct, though. 'I am the sole heir to the Tulano throne. The people have been patient long enough.'

'But how do you *feel*?'

'I prefer not to feel,' Rafe said. 'Feelings tend to complicate things.'

'So you choose not to have them?'

'Yes.'

Only that wasn't strictly true, for walking and talking with Antonietta gave him a feeling he would like to capture and store. This morning, walking free, with the winter sun high and Antonietta by his side, his life felt exhilarating rather than complicated.

'And the women you…' she swallowed '…you date? Are you saying that you don't have feelings for them?'

'I am not a machine,' Rafe said. 'Nor am I an utter bastard.' He looked sideways and saw that her head was down. She was frowning slightly as she tried to understand him. 'It is said by many that I have my father's heart…'

Antonietta flushed, because Aurora had said much the same thing. 'And do you?'

'No,' Rafe said. 'I have my mother's heart. I don't get close to people, Antonietta. I am cold like that.'

'Is she cold to you?'

'Especially to me. My parents were young when they married and I think she blames my arrival for my father's philandering ways. She is the epitome of the Ice Queen.'

'Perhaps so—but *I* don't find you cold, Rafe.'

'Because you haven't seen me when I choose to move on. Then I am as detached and indifferent as she. That is why I prefer to pay for company; that is why I choose to have a contract.'

'Yet I haven't signed anything.'

'No.' He gave a tight smile at this.

'So what if I go to the press?' Antonietta asked. 'What if in a couple of years' time I'm on some chat show, revealing all?'

'All?' Rafe checked. 'You mean you would tell the world about the night I took your virginity…?'

He loved it that she blushed, and he loved it that he knew she would never reveal it, and yet he teased her all the same.

'Would you tell them about the morning I took you in the temple ruins…?'

'You didn't, though,' she said, even as he pulled her towards him. 'And you won't—we can be seen from the monastery.'

'If people have binoculars,' Rafe pointed out, but as he moved in to kiss her he could taste her tension and feel her distraction, so he halted their kiss and held her a moment.

Rafe thought of how happy she had been when they'd been away from here. How the tension had lifted from her shoulders, how she had laughed and danced and relaxed in his arms. He thought of his yacht, and the privacy that would be afforded them there.

And he decided.

'Come with me to Capri.'

CHAPTER NINE

HE MADE IT HAPPEN.

Antonietta waited at the cottage while Rafe headed off to change. She would have loved to do the same, but apart from her red silk dress there weren't many options.

She pulled on some tights, and her most comfortable boots for all the sightseeing ahead, and decided she would just have to do.

By the time Rafe returned, dressed in black jeans and a jumper topped with a fine grey woollen coat, his helicopter was out of the hangar.

Antonietta had only ever heard the choppers, or seen them arriving and leaving, but now she sat in Rafe's private one, her stomach lurching as it lifted into the sky.

Capri was well known for the capricious nature of its weather, but it turned on the sun today, and the ocean was azure beneath them.

She stared at the white cliffs as they approached the island.

'There it is…' Rafe spoke to her through headphones and pointed down to his yacht in Marina Grande—possibly the most exclusive marina in the world.

But Antonietta was not looking at it. 'I've always wanted to see the Christmas decorations in Capri,' she said, with her hands pressed to the window. 'And to eat *struffoli*. I can't believe you've brought me here!'

They were not in Capri to see the Christmas lights and eat *struffoli*, Rafe thought to himself. He had brought them here for the opulent privacy of his yacht and an awful lot of sex.

Yet his self-proclaimed cold indifference seemed to elude him around Antonietta, and he did not want to disappoint her.

As if his yacht had ever disappointed!

But Antonietta clearly thought they were here on some sort of day trip, so a word was had with his pilot in rapid French, and Rafe had to quickly rethink their day…

'You'll freeze in what you're wearing,' he told her as they sat in a sumptuous café and shared a plate of the famous *struffoli*. 'You need to get something warmer to wear.'

'I'll be fine.'

'We're going out to the Blue Grotto,' Rafe said. He'd go anywhere if it meant getting her out of those appalling tights—and for once he wasn't thinking about sex. 'You'll need to rug up.'

'It's closed in December,' she told him, for she had heard the tourists on the next table grumbling about it.

'It's not closed for me.'

And so they headed to Via Camerelle, with its designer boutiques, and he sipped coffee and insisted that the pale grey woollen dress that hugged her slender frame required a coat, and boots in the softest suede.

'And you'll need a dress and shoes for to-night,' Rafe told her.

'I have to be back at work tomorrow,' she told him.

'And you shall be,' Rafe told her. 'Get a dress.'

He told her he had an appointment to keep, and suggested that while she waited for him she might as well get her hair done.

'Rafe,' Antonietta protested. 'Please don't try to change me.'

'I don't want to change you,' Rafe said. 'But I have never known a woman to turn down a couple of hours in a salon in Via Vittorio Emanuele just to wait in a car.'

The suited men were back. Hovering discreetly, but annoyingly present. And Antonietta could tell they were less than pleased with her.

So, yes, she chose to get her hair done—rather than sit in a car with a driver who looked at her through slightly narrowed eyes.

That was the very reason Rafe needed some time away from her. He headed to the private royal residence for a less than straightforward meeting with his aides and minders, who were all appalled that he had brought a woman onto shore. Not just that, the same woman who had been in the August Suite the other night.

'She has not been vetted,' his advisor warned. 'And you still haven't had her sign the NDA.'

Neither would he. For this was too precious. And he told them none too gently to back off, and that he would deal with the fallout that would inevitably come from a run-in with the King.

It was worth it for this.

Antonietta's long, straight dark hair was still long, straight and dark, but just a vital inch shorter, and so glossy and thick that he put up a hand just to feel it.

And then he looked into dark eyes that were painted smoky and seductive. He took the coat from the doorman, just so he could help her into it himself, and handed her expensive shades.

'Wear these,' he suggested, 'if you don't want people at work to know.'

For Crown Prince Rafael was in Capri, and there was a stir in all the best restaurants, where they put a 'reserved' sign on their very best table in the hope that he might dine there tonight. And in the cobbled streets the locals soon heard that the Playboy Prince had a woman on his arm.

'Who is she?' they asked—because usually Rafe did not bring his dates in from his yacht, where he tended to party. Perhaps he was finally serious about someone.

His luxurious yacht would not fit into the

Blue Grotto cove, of course, so a speedboat took them in. There they transferred to a small wooden row-boat with a single skipper.

'We'll have to lie down,' Rafe told her.

'Really?' she checked, unsure if he was teasing.

'Really.'

He wasn't joking, but she wouldn't have minded if he had been, for it was bliss to lie side by side with him.

And then they entered the grotto. And it was like sliding into heaven as they were bathed in sapphire light.

'It's wonderful…' Antonietta breathed, for the water and its reflection was magical, the cavern illuminated spectacularly. And today, just for them, music was playing, inviting them further in. 'I've never seen anything more beautiful.'

'Nor have I,' Rafe told her.

And she decided that even though he might have used that line many times she would let that thought go. For when he looked at her like that, when he kissed her so slowly, she felt like the only girl in his world. She felt as if she belonged.

Rafe felt Antonietta still in his arms and, concerned, he halted. 'Is everything okay?'

'Yes,' she answered.

And all those years of searching, and yearning, and never quite fitting in, ended then, and she found her place in the world in his arms.

Oh, it made no logical sense, for it was not about the *place* she was in, it was the connection she had found.

Only then did she understand what Aurora had meant when she had advised her to let go of her heart. For letting go meant no thoughts of tomorrow and a cold, indifferent end. And to let go meant she didn't examine the impossibility of them. She just had to let her heart go and it would fly straight to Rafe.

'Keep kissing me.'

'I can do that,' Rafe said.

He kissed her so deep and so long and with such smouldering passion that she felt as if she were floating, and that if he let go of her she might rise to the ceiling of the cove.

But even Blue Grotto kisses must end.

It was cold and getting dark when he held out his hand and helped her into the speedboat.

Instead of going to his yacht, they headed to shore.

The Christmas lights of Capri were truly an amazing sight—not that he'd really paid attention before. They strolled through the square, with its carpets of fairy lights on the buildings and in canopies above them. It was like walking through a nativity scene, with towering musical trees draped in a million lights.

'This is the best day of my life,' Antonietta told him. 'The best Christmas.'

For *this* was her Christmas she decided. Tonight, here with Rafe.

It was cold, though, and their time on the water and the salty ocean breeze meant that not even his arm around her and her new thick coat could keep her from shivering.

'Let's go and eat,' Rafe said.

'I want *ravioli caprese* while I'm here,' Antonietta said, 'and chocolate torte…'

Any restaurant in Capri would serve that. And all the best restaurants, he knew, would have a table reserved for them.

Yet he was sick to the back teeth of restaurants.

There was somewhere else he wanted to take Antonietta.

'Come on, then.'

He called for his driver, and as he saw Antonietta into the vehicle he told the driver where they were headed.

The driver asked him to repeat the location.

'You heard,' Rafe said, although he knew it was *un*heard of for him to take a date to one of his family's private residences.

They drove slowly up a hill and then turned in at a concealed entrance. She peered out of the darkened windows for a sign that might tell her the name of the restaurant he had chosen, but there wasn't one. Antonietta looked over to Rafe for an explanation as some gates slid open and they drove slowly up a steep path canopied in trees.

'Where are we going?'

'My family has a private residence here.'

'You *family*?' she croaked. 'They won't be here?'

'Of course not,' Rafe said. 'I thought it might be pleasanter than a restaurant.'

Antonietta wasn't so sure… A polite greeting

awaited them, but she could sense the caution in the staff when they arrived.

The entrance to the villa was vast, with high vaulted ceilings that seemed to shrink her as they stepped inside. Rafe took off his coat and handed it to the butler, who waited for Antonietta to do the same.

Rafe could feel her discomfort as she handed over her coat and was already ruing his decision to bring her here as he led her through to the lounge.

A huge fire was waiting, and Antonietta stood and warmed her hands as the butler poured drinks.

'They must have been expecting you,' she said, referring to the fire and the fleet of staff. 'But from their surprise I thought you had arrived unannounced.'

The surprise was Antonietta.

Not that he told her.

'They are used to me arriving at all hours,' Rafe said. 'I'm sorry if it feels awkward to be here. I never thought…'

'No,' Antonietta said. 'I'm glad to be here. I'm just…'

She was just overwhelmed—not by her surroundings, but by the fact that he had brought her here. The fact that this man, who had told her he was cold, had lit a flame in her heart. How this man, who was a prince, somehow made her feel not just equal but as if she had found her missing part.

'I'm hungry!' she said, because that felt safe.

'Then let's get dressed for dinner.'

They climbed the stairs, and it felt so different from the monastery—for, no matter how luxurious, that was still a hotel. This was a home, with pictures lining the stairwell, and though it might be one of many homes there were personal touches that no hotel could replicate.

When she stepped into his bedroom it was Rafe's books upon the shelves and his chosen artwork on the walls.

And there was *his* bed.

A high, ornate, dark wooden bed, dressed in jade velvet. She couldn't resist sitting on the edge and bouncing up and down. It felt as delicious as it looked.

He took her leg and removed one of her gorgeous suede boots.

'I would love to sleep here,' she said.

She wanted to know what it was like to sleep in Rafe's own bed, and to know a little more of his life.

'Then do.'

'I have to be back for work,' she reminded him as he removed the other boot. 'I have a shift in the Oratory.'

But she forgot about work after that, liking how deftly he undressed her, lifting her bottom as he removed her stockings, and her panties too, and then pushed her shoulders down so she toppled back onto the mattress.

She lifted up onto her elbows and watched as he parted her legs and exposed her. And then examined her with desirous eyes. She should be shy, Antonietta thought. Yet she was not.

There was no kiss, no preamble. And her legs were pliant, rather than resisting, as Rafe placed them over his wide shoulders.

'I *have* to taste you,' Rafe said.

'Then do.'

He had been right to bring her here. Rafe

knew it then. She deserved better than exposed temple grounds, and she did not need the ghosts of his past on the yacht, nor another nameless hotel, Rafe thought as he parted legs that were still cold from their day out.

She was warm *there* though.

He looked at her glistening folds and all he could do was taste…

Antonietta did not know, had not even imagined, that a mouth could deliver such bliss. His unshaven jaw was rough, and though his tongue was soft it made her feel exquisitely tender. There was no desire to pull away. He tasted her slowly and leisurely as her heart seemed to beat in her throat. He explored her more thoroughly, just a little roughly, and her thighs trembled as he tasted her deeply, dizzied her with light suction, then with decadent flicks with his tongue.

And never—not once—did she ask him to stop.

He was probing, and thorough and she found that she was panting, desperate—but for what she didn't quite know. Her hands went up and grasped at the bedcover, but it kept slipping away, like her own control.

'Rafe!' she pleaded—except she didn't know for what she was pleading.

She was back in the Blue Grotto on the crystalline waters. She was floating again, yet held by his mouth. She could hear her own voice calling his name as her fingers knotted in his thick hair.

He moaned into her, and his mouth was more insistent now. He was kneeling up and pulling her deeper into him. There was nowhere to go and nowhere to hide from the bliss he delivered. Every nerve in her body seemed arrowed to her centre, every beat of her heart felt aimed at her sex—until she sobbed and shattered and pulsed to his skilled mouth.

And he tasted her all through it. Even as her orgasm was fading he tenderly caressed those last flickers from her and then knelt back.

His swallow was the most intimate sound she had ever heard.

Antonietta dressed for dinner in the silver-grey dress she had bought earlier that day, then sat at the large dressing table and got ready. Her hair fell into perfect shape as she ran a silver comb through it and Aurora's red lipstick was worn again.

Rafe had never known a woman to take so little time to get dressed for dinner and to look so breathtaking when she did. But it was not the dress, nor the hair that had transformed her. It was the sparkle in her eyes, Rafe realised, and he felt proud that he had brought joy to her.

'You look amazing,' he told her.

'Thank you.' She smiled and then added, 'You *always* do.'

And never more so than now. Rafe had shaved, his raven hair was brushed back, and he had changed into a deep navy suit.

She understood better the merits of dressing for dinner, for she felt a certain thrill that he had dressed so smartly, so immaculately, even though they were not to be seen, for they were not going out. Rafe had shaved and dressed with care only for *her*.

He took her up to a moonlit terrace, looking out to the Faraglioni rock formations. They sat at a beautifully dressed table, under burners that kept them as warm as a real fire.

'I can't believe I'm here,' Antonietta said.

'I can,' Rafe said.

It felt right.

Dinner was served, and somehow it was an intimate affair, and she gasped when *ravioli caprese* arrived.

'How did the chef know?'

'I told him,' Rafe said. 'Though we might have to wait a little while for the chocolate torte.'

'I don't mind waiting,' Antonietta said. Then asked, 'Do you come here a lot?'

'Not often,' Rafe said. 'My father uses it as a retreat, but I tend to give it a miss and stay out on my yacht.' He saw her slight frown. 'Growing up, I would come here sometimes in summer.'

'With your family?'

'No. My mother felt holidays were pointless. I came here with the nanny, and later I would bring friends.' He gave a wry smile. 'Vetted, of course.'

'But I am not vetted.'

'You have been by me,' Rafe said. 'And I like everything I see.'

'You have my discretion.'

'I know that.' And for the first time in his life he really did.

'This has been the perfect day.'

'An unplanned day,' Rafe admitted. 'I was going to take you to my yacht, but then you said you wanted to see the Christmas lights and eat *struffoli*...'

'You were taking me to your *yacht*?' Antonietta checked. 'For what? Sex?'

'And fine dining.' Rafe smiled. 'Thankfully, I realised just in time that you wanted a day trip.'

And now he had been so honest, she could be honest too. 'I just wanted a day with you, Rafe.'

Well, she'd got it. Rafe had given her a perfect day. And yet the moon moved too fast behind the clouds, and their time together was slipping away.

Dessert was served, and it was delicious—especially when fed to her from his silver spoon.

The second Rafe dismissed the staff she slipped from her side of the table to his knee and they tasted each other again.

She wanted his bed. His velvet bed. She wanted to lie there tonight and to wake with him tomorrow and for their time together to never end.

'We should head back,' Rafe told her. 'If you *have* to be at work.'

She heard the unsubtle emphasis.

'I do,' Antonietta said. 'I can't let them down…'

Rafe would be gone soon, and right now work was the only constant she had.

'I have to get back.'

'I know that.'

'But not yet…'

Not before he took her to his velvet bed.

CHAPTER TEN

ANTONIETTA WASN'T LATE, EXACTLY.

The helicopter pilot made excellent time and they arrived just before the winter sun rose above the horizon—which gave Antonietta just enough time for a quick shower and to change, though she was cutting it fine.

There was no morning chat with Pino.

Antonietta had got away with it.

Rafe hadn't.

Before he had even shrugged out of his coat his father was on the phone. The call was neither unexpected nor pleasant.

'What the hell were you thinking, parading this woman in Capri?' his father demanded.

'Hardly "parading",' Rafe said. 'It hasn't even made the papers.' He knew, because while Antonietta had been dozing beside him on the flight home he'd checked.

'Only because your PR team have been working all night to silence it.' The King was incensed. 'You are supposed to be recovering—'

'I am fully recovered,' Rafe interrupted.

'Then come home.'

'I'm not due back until Christmas Eve.'

'That wasn't a suggestion, Rafe. You have been given an extremely generous length of rope, yet you choose to ignore all the conditions that come with it. Well, no more. You are to return home. And in the New Year there shall be an announcement as to your upcoming marriage. The party is over, Rafe.'

'I am in no position to get engaged,' Rafe answered curtly. 'As you are clearly aware, I am currently seeing someone.'

It was more than he had wanted to reveal—more than he had even acknowledged to himself. But the fact was he was more involved with Antonietta than he had ever been or intended to be with anyone.

'Then *un*see her,' the King said.

Rafe walked out onto the balcony and there, crossing the grounds, was Antonietta. She was dressed in a white uniform and tying her hair back as she walked briskly to begin her shift.

'It's not that straightforward—'

'Are you forgetting who you are conversing with?' his father cut in.

For a moment Rafe had. But he was not under the thumb of his parents—it was the full weight of his title that came crashing down as the King spoke on.

'Your accident caused great concern, Rafe. You have a responsibility to marry and to produce heirs.'

'It is too soon,' Rafe said.

He was not even thinking of himself—more of Antonietta finding out he was engaged a few days after they'd ended.

'As I said, I am seeing someone, and she—'

'*She* has no bearing on this discussion,' the King said. '*She* is a lowly maid, who has been disowned by her own family because of a chequered past…'

'Don't even *go* there!' Rafe shouted.

'I should say the same to you,' his father shot back. 'Rafe, if you are particularly enamoured of this woman, then after your marriage, after an appropriate length of time, you can discreetly—'

'Don't!' Rafe interrupted, and his voice was low and threatening, even if his father was the King. 'Don't even try to give me relationship advice or instruct me on how to conduct my marriage.'

'Again, I remind you of to whom you are speaking,' the King said. 'I shall grant you this day to conclude matters and then I expect your return to the palace this night.'

The King had spoken and he was calling him home.

It was a busy day in the Oratory. As Antonietta had predicted, a lot of the guests had saved their treatments to be taken close to Christmas. And even if Christmas was a somewhat muted affair out in the main building, here in the Oratory it was festive indeed.

She painted many nails red and even performed her first massage on a paying client.

'Busy day?' Pino asked, long after six, when the last client had finally left.

'Very.' She sighed. 'How about you?'

'Lots of activity…' He halted. 'Never mind.'

It would seem that Pino had found his discretion button. 'Ready for Christmas?'

'Pretty much.'

'Is that for Aurora?' Pino asked, when she showed him the large bottle of fragrant oil she had purchased with her staff discount.

It was easier to nod—though of course it was for Rafe. Antonietta had decided that chocolate wasn't enough, and had been racking her brains as to what she could get him. What was a person supposed to buy for a prince who had everything?

Including her heart.

She had let go of her heart and lost it to Blue Grotto kisses, and now she had spent half a week's wages on a bottle of neroli oil and had it wrapped in a bow.

Antonietta had never been happier in her life and it had not gone unnoticed—even Pino commented now that she looked brighter.

'I'm just…' But Antonietta could not explain the joy that radiated from her, nor her sudden exuberance, for fraternising with guests was strictly forbidden. So she blamed the season of goodwill for her wide smile. 'Looking forward to Christmas, I guess.'

Which was a lie, because she was actually dreading it, for by Christmas Rafe would be gone.

'Only four more days,' Pino said, and then his phone started to ring. 'Do you mind if I get that? It's my daughter—she's with the in-laws and worried about me.'

'Sure.' Antonietta smiled. 'Say hi from me.'

He gave her a wave and as she stepped into the night she saw that Pino was huddled over his phone, with his back to her, engrossed in his conversation.

There were no guests coming in or out to concern him. No cars arriving or helicopters approaching, nor guests checking in or out.

She could walk the fifteen minutes it would take her to get home, quickly get changed, and then walk the fifteen minutes back to Rafe's suite's private entrance.

Or she could go there now and have an extra thirty-five minutes with him.

And when you only had three days until Christmas Eve, when the man you were falling for was leaving, those minutes counted. And so, instead of walking home, Antonietta walked back inside the monastery.

If Pino saw her she would say she had left her phone, or something.

But there was no need for the excuses she had practised, for so deep in conversation was Pino that she entered unseen, slipped behind the stone partition and took the elevator without being spotted.

Past the Starlight and Temple Suites and through the cloister she walked briskly, wondering which excuse she would give if she was caught.

There was no guard on the door, and Antonietta frowned, because she had never known Rafe's suite to be unattended. And it was not just his suite that was unguarded. As she swiped her card and pushed the door open Antonietta realised that her heart was unguarded too.

For almost the first time since his arrival she *hadn't* spent the day with her ears strained for the sound of his helicopter, signalling that he was leaving. Or for Francesca's voice informing her that Signor Dupont had departed and she should turn over his suite.

And now she stood there, silent and completely unprepared, for she held his gift in her hands and her face still bore the smile she had been wearing when she entered, as if the wind had changed and set it there.

An ill wind.

When she had expected it least, Rafe had gone.

'Antonietta!'

She jumped at the sound of her name, and as Rafe flicked on the light he frowned, for her face was alabaster-white.

'You're early.'

'I didn't go home.' Her voice was strained and she cleared her throat. 'I came straight here. Why are you in darkness?'

'I was taking a shower.'

And that made sense, for he wore nothing more than a towel, but the fire wasn't even lit.

'There's no guard on the door.'

'No,' Rafe said, and he could see the questions in her eyes.

To avoid them, he turned and lit the fire. The

guards had not just been there for his protection, they had reported back to the King. And they were not mere 'guards', they were Royal Protection Officers, which meant they were completely within their brief to carry out background checks on her. And when he had told them to leave they had retreated only to the perimeter of the hotel.

But his senior RPO, who had worked with Rafe for years, had stayed back, warning him that he should be back in Tulano by now, by request of the King.

It had been one step down from an order.

'I'm aware of that,' Rafe had told him. 'This is my doing.'

His doing.

'Antonietta…' he started, and loathed the austerity of his tone—but it was surely kinder in the long run, and there was no point prettying up his words.

'I got you a present…' she said.

He glanced down at the bottle she held, dressed in a red velvet bow.

'That was not necessary,' Rafe said.

'Presents shouldn't be *necessary*.' Antonietta

smiled, but it wavered. 'It was just something I saw…'

Rafe was more than used to gifts. So *very* used to them. But none had ever shot to his heart in the way this did.

Not only could she not afford it, but it had been chosen with care, and he was loath to cause offence.

'Thank you,' he said.

'Smell it.'

He would rather not, and yet she was already unscrewing the lid.

Rather than offering him the bottle, she poured some into her palm and held out her hand for him to sniff.

'I was worried about your shoulder,' Antonietta said, and attempted to place her oiled hand there, feeling him actually wince at her uninvited fingers, while berating herself for thinking she could possibly spoil a man who could have anything he wanted.

Even her.

'It's too cold in here, though,' Antonietta said, and removed her hand.

She wasn't referring to the temperature of the

room. Even though she had tried to ignore it, she could pick up his resistant vibe.

And she refused to beg.

'Enjoy,' she said, and placed the bottle on the table.

Unsure of him for the first time, she turned to go.

'Antonietta.' He caught her oiled hand but it slipped from his grasp, so he caught her more firmly and turned her around to face him. 'Don't leave.'

'I don't feel very welcome all of a sudden.'

'You are *always* welcome.'

He took her hand and placed it back on his shoulder. The contact was her undoing, for she had craved this moment for so much longer than today.

His bruises had all but gone, though there were still two dark lines where the rotator cuff had sheared, and now, when he winced at her touch, it was not in recoil more in targeted relief.

'Did I hurt you that night on the dance floor?' Antonietta asked, and she watched his arrogant mouth edge into a smile.

'A bit,' he said. 'And then you dug your nails into me when we were in bed...'

'I don't have long nails,' Antonietta said, and she pressed her fingers in, exactly where it would hurt.

He sucked in his breath and then exhaled as the muscle was released. 'They felt like long nails,' Rafe said.

He was already hardening, and turned on, and his resolution to avoid break-up sex was fading.

'What pain we both felt that night,' Antonietta said. 'When you took me I thought I might die.'

And as she took him back to that moment Rafe knew that he, the practised seducer, was being seduced by the shy maid with the sad eyes. It was he who had brought this side out in her, Rafe lamented, and he felt a snap of possessiveness at the thought of her out in the world without him. It was a coil in his gut that was unfamiliar as her fingers dug and pressed and kneaded.

She traced a finger around his flat mahogany nipples and then nipped him there with her teeth.

'Antonietta…'

She lifted her head and looked right at him. There was no trace of sadness, and nor was she shy, but he could not bring himself to do what he must and end it.

And so he ripped open the poppers of her white therapist's uniform and scooped her breasts from their flimsy bra. He took some of the oil and warmed it in his palm before playing with them, at first gently, then increasingly roughly.

His towel was gone, and he pushed her dress down over her arms and down past her hips. She stepped out of her knickers along with the rest of her clothes.

Once they were naked, Rafe pulled them both down to the floor and lifted her hips. It was her hand that guided him as he slipped into her tight space. And they were panting and hot on this cool December night, as he held her hips so he could fill her with his thick length.

Antonietta was up on her knees, holding onto his oiled and slippery shoulders, watching the delicious sight of him sliding in and out of her. Her hair was on his face, and as he brushed it back their mouths met in frenzied, swollen kisses.

They both knew they must stop.

But he could feel her abandon and he craved just a little more.

'We should…' He attempted to speak. He knew he ought to lift her off him, for the protection was in the master bedroom. Except there was no going back now. The condoms might as well be locked in a vault in Switzerland for all the hope he had of getting to them.

He grew careless, as he never had before. It was unthinkable that he should have unprotected sex—not least because Antonietta wasn't on the Pill. But it was *such* a building need… And he *had* to feel her come around him.

'Rafe…'

She delivered her warning that she was close and he hit the snooze button on his thoughts, sinking into the flickering bliss of her grip.

She felt the final swell of him and yelped as he crashed over the edge and lost himself in the hot pulse of her tender flesh.

So careless. Because now he ignored the world outside, and the conversation that needed to be had, and carried her to his bed.

Everything else could wait.

CHAPTER ELEVEN

FOR ONCE, ANTONIETTA was up long *after* the Silibri sun.

Dizzy from lack of sleep, they had crashed at dawn.

Last night Rafe had hit the proverbial snooze button on his mental alarm.

This morning Antonietta had hit the real one.

Outside the warm bed the room was cold, so it had been easy—too easy—to give in to the arm that pulled her into his warmth and drift back to sleep.

'Shall I open the drapes for you, Signor Dupont?'

The sound of Francesca's voice jolted Antonietta awake, although her eyes did not open. Rafe's hand tightened on her bare arm and she lay as if set in stone, with her heart fluttering like a trapped bird in her chest.

'No,' Rafe said. 'That will be all.' And then he added, 'Thank you.'

Antonietta heard the bedroom door close and it felt like for ever until the main door opened and shut. Only then did she sit up and let out a low moan. 'Francesca knew I was here.'

'Of course she didn't. You could have been anyone,' Rafe said. 'The lights are not on…'

'No,' Antonietta said. 'Francesca is the manager. She doesn't bring guests their coffee—not even royal ones. She *knew* I was here…'

'How?'

'She's been checking on me.'

Antonietta climbed out of bed, pulled a throw from the top of it and wrapped it around her. 'That day when she suddenly came to check your suite with me…'

'You're reading too much into things,' Rafe said with stoic calm even as she dashed into the lounge.

'No, Rafe, I'm not.'

Francesca knew—of that Antonietta was certain.

'Did you fold my uniform after you removed it from me?' Antonietta asked as he joined her in the lounge. 'Did you carefully place it over the chair?'

His hand came down on her shoulder and he turned her to face him. Of course he had not.

He wrapped her in a strong embrace. Her head was on his chest and she listened to the steady *thud, thud, thud* of his heart and wished hers could match it.

'I will speak with Nico,' Rafe said.

'No,' Antonietta said. 'I don't need you to do me any favours. I will handle it myself.' She pulled her head from his chest.

'You don't have to.'

'Of course I do.' She removed herself from the haven of his arms. 'How can your intervening possibly help? You weren't the one caught—that was me…'

'Antonietta…' Rafe attempted reason. 'It was both of us.'

'No.' She shook her head. 'You can sleep with whomever you choose, Rafe.' She gave him a tight smile. 'And from everything I've heard you frequently do.'

'Don't do this, Antonietta,' Rafe warned. 'Don't turn this into something cheap.'

But in her head Antonietta already had.

She had struggled to justify sleeping with Rafe even to herself, while all the time knowing that it could go nowhere. In the cold light of day she saw it was impossible to defend it now—especially to others.

She showered quickly and then dressed in her uniform, and came out to find Rafe lying on the bed with his hands behind his head, looking grim.

'I don't blame *you*,' Antonietta said, 'I should have set the alarm…'

'Why does blame have to be apportioned?' Rafe asked.

'Because we are in Silibri,' Antonietta said. 'Finding someone to blame is our national sport.'

'Antonietta,' Rafe said. 'I won't let you lose your job because of me…'

Damn, he hadn't even told her he was leaving today.

'I've lost more than my job to you, Rafe.'

'You speak as if you were an unwilling participant.' His voice came out defensive and derisive, as it tended to when he was feeling caught out.

'I'm talking about my virginity,' Antonietta replied, loathing her own tone, but she felt caught out too.

He didn't know what to do as she flounced off. His immediate thought was to call Nico and put in a word, but he knew she would hate that. Or he could head down and apologise to Francesca…

Rafe felt as if he was back at school.

And then the weight of his own problems arrived at his door.

Antonietta would have barely made it through the cloister when there came a heavy knock.

It was his RPO, looking grim. 'You are to call the palace.'

'I have already spoken with the King,' Rafe responded tartly. He did not need to be told again that it was time for him to leave.

But he had not understood the message.

'It is the Queen who wishes to speak with you.'

Rafe could not remember a time when his mother had requested to speak with him, and for a moment he felt ice run down his spine. It must be bad news. His mother never called. Not during his schooling, nor when he was injured.

So rare was this request that by the time he had been put through to the palace Rafe had almost convinced himself that his father must be on his deathbed and he was about to become King.

Not now, Rafe thought. *Not like this.*

'Rafael.'

His mother's tone gave him no clue—it was brusque and efficient as always.

'I spoke with your father at length last night.'

'He is well?' Rafe checked.

'Of course he is.' Marcelle sounded irritated. 'Rafe, I understand you are involved with someone?'

'Yes.'

'I have heard your father's poor advice to you.'

For a second he thought he had an ally. That possibly his mother was on his side. But this was not a gentle lead-in. There was no preamble with the Ice Queen.

'End things with her and do it immediately.'

'That's your advice?'

'Of course,' Marcelle said. 'Or would you prefer your father's suggestion to keep her on call? It *is* doable, of course,' Marcelle said. 'I should know.'

Rafe drew in a breath and found that he was holding it. His mother had never discussed his father's ways. At least not with Rafe.

'You took her to Capri?' Marcelle checked.

'I did.'

'You can take her there again…'

Rafe frowned.

'But I will tell you this much, Rafe,' his mother said. 'Your wife must never set foot on that island.'

Rafe had always found his mother cold. In that moment he knew she burnt with humiliation and pain.

'I would never do that to my wife.'

'Good,' Marcelle said. 'Because right now your future wife is being chosen and your engagement is to be announced on New Year's Day. Do as I suggest, and end it with this woman cleanly and quietly. Leave her in no doubt that the two of you are completely through.'

* * *

For Antonietta it was quite a walk of shame to Francesca's office.

Yes, she had lost more than her virginity to Rafe. She had lost her pride. For there was little pride to be salvaged when you were found in an eminent guest's bed. But more than that she had lost her heart to Rafe, and that was the part that hurt the most.

It came to her then that this would never have happened had she not been falling in love.

She pressed her eyes closed on that thought as she knocked at Francesca's door.

'Come in.'

Francesca's voice was hostile and so were her eyes as Antonietta stepped in and closed the door.

'Are you here to deliver your resignation?' Francesca asked.

'No,' Antonietta said. 'I am here to apologise. I know it looks terrible, but—'

'Don't make excuses,' Francesca broke in. 'It is forbidden for staff to fraternise or offer favours to guests for reward. Signor Caruso is very clear on that fact.'

'Yes, but I was not offering favours. Aurora knows and—'

'Oh, that's right—you are friends with the boss's wife.' Francesca again cut her off. 'Very well. You can tell your friend that Nico shall have my resignation by lunchtime.'

'No,' Antonietta protested. 'Why would you leave because of me?'

The very thought that Francesca would resign over this appalled Antonietta, who knew the manager loved her work. Francesca worked both day and night, greeting their most esteemed guests, ensuring that every detail of their stay was perfect. She couldn't understand why her actions might force Francesca out.

'If I'd wanted to be a madam then I would have applied for a job at Rubina's.'

Rubina's was the bordello in the next village.

'I am not a whore,' Antonietta said. 'I am not being paid or anything like that…'

'Oh, *please*,' Francesca sneered. 'I don't believe you for a moment.'

'But it's true,' Antonietta insisted, and then admitted a truth she had been trying to resist until now. 'It has nothing to do with money. I love him.'

There was silence from both of them at the enormity of her words, for Francesca knew that Antonietta was not one for passionate declarations.

'Oh, Antonietta…' Francesca sighed. 'You foolish, foolish girl.'

But she said it kindly, and Antonietta knew that Francesca really cared. In truth, she ached for a more mature woman's advice. 'Why foolish?'

'I thought that you at least knew what you were doing and that it was a business arrangement.'

'You'd rather that he was paying me?'

'Yes,' Francesca admitted. 'I'd rather that than you give your heart to a man who is using you.'

'But he *isn't* using me.'

'No—you offered yourself to him on a plate.'

She had.

Antonietta's eyes screwed closed as realisation started to hit and she recalled that first night, outside her cottage, and her reaction to her very first kiss. *Take me to bed.* It had felt at the time as necessary and straightforward as that.

'Sit down, Antonietta,' Francesca said gently.

She offered tissues, and poured water, and then pulled her chair around so she sat next to Antonietta.

The older woman took her hand. 'I won't tell anyone, and neither will I lose my job over this, or you yours, but there is a condition.'

'What?'

'You are to go and tell Signor Dupont—or rather, Crown Prince Rafael—that you have kept your job only on the condition that, after your conversation, you will never speak to him again.'

Antonietta swallowed.

'You are not to be in his suite and he is not to come to your home. There will be no more contact between the two of you.'

'But—'

Francesca spoke over her. 'And after you tell him that I can guarantee that within hours he will leave. Crown Prince Rafael was not expected to stay here for even a few days. I was told that as soon as he was even partway healed he would grow bored and fly out.'

'He didn't leave, though.'

'Of course not. He was getting sex and nightly entertainment. Tell me, Antonietta, why *would* he leave?'

'It wasn't like that—'

'It was *exactly* like that, and I should know,' Francesca said. 'I was taken advantage of by a man a year after my husband left me. I'm guessing that you were lonely?'

Antonietta opened her mouth to argue, but the truth was she *had* been lonely—desperately so. 'Yes,' she admitted. 'But Rafe did not take advantage of that fact. I was complicit.'

'You were out of your depth,' Francesca countered. 'He is a notorious playboy. Have you not seen him in the scandal rags?' Francesca answered her own question. 'Of course not—you wouldn't read them. But, Antonietta, not all gossip is bad. It can serve as a warning.'

'I doubt I would have heeded any warning.'

Antonietta thought back and knew that there might have been a group of protesters on the lawn that first night, as she had walked to his suite, and they could have been holding placards attesting to his reputation, and still she would not have let go of his hand.

'He told me from the start it could go nowhere…'

'Of course not.'

'Even before I knew who he was.'

'And now that you do, be the one to end it.'

Francesca gave her shy and somewhat naive chambermaid a little cuddle, and felt angry on her behalf—and not just with Prince Rafael.

'Antonietta, for what it is worth, I will not tell your mother.'

'I don't care any more.'

She would have dreaded that a short while ago, but no longer. She had spent these last years frozen at age twenty-one, desperate to reclaim their approval.

'I cannot keep apologising for being me.'

'No,' Francesca said. 'And neither should you. I think your parents' treatment of you has been terrible and I have told your mother the same. We are no longer speaking.'

'I'm sorry.'

'No more saying sorry,' Francesca said.

'One more apology,' Antonietta replied.

In the last hour she had learnt many lessons, and she now felt all of her twenty-six years. She knew that Francesca was being stern out of kindness and to protect her.

'I will always be Aurora's best friend, but I will never use that friendship again. At work, I answer only to you.'

'Thank you,' Francesca said.

It felt right. And for a moment the world felt a lot better than it had in recent years. But now came the hard part. The hardest part.

To let Rafe go with grace and not let him see the agony in her heart.

Antonietta knocked on the door, and instead of being called to come in, or using her swipe card, this time Rafe opened it.

He wore black jeans and a black shirt and was unshaven, yet somehow he seemed so immaculate and regal that Antonietta wondered how she had not known he was royal on sight.

'Come in,' Rafe said. 'How did you get on?'

'Okay, I think,' Antonietta said.

And because she felt as if her knees might

give way she chose to take a seat opposite the chair on which Francesca had folded her uniform dress, on the sofa on which they had made love the previous evening.

'I have assured her that it will never happen again.'

'You are hardly going to make a habit of sleeping with the guests.'

'I think she understands that it won't happen again. And I won't be coming to your suite again.'

Rafe actually opened his mouth to dispute that. To wave his royal wand, or rather have things smoothed over, but to what end?

He was leaving, and it was far better to end it now. Cleanly. He did not want to follow his father's example.

Rafe glimpsed it then—a future for them of the kind his father had described. He could return to Silibri at every whim. Take out a permanent lease on the August Suite…

No. Better he followed his mother's example and killed this now.

Or let her think that she had.

'Perhaps that would be for the best.' His voice was steady and he watched her rapid blinking.

'So I'm dismissed?' Antonietta could not keep the hurt at his cold reply from her voice.

'You are the one saying that you won't be returning to my suite,' Rafe pointed out. 'You are the one saying that you cannot see me any more.'

'Yes, but…' She had hoped for some protest, some indication—*any* indication—that this was hurting him even a fraction of how much it was killing her. Yet he seemed unmoved.

'I told you this could go nowhere.'

'You did, but…'

That *but* again. He could hear her attempting to defend them. Worse, he was still glimpsing that future.

And so he killed it, with brutal but necessary words, for he could not drag it out any longer. 'I am to marry,' Rafe said. 'My engagement will be announced in the New Year.'

'Why are you telling me this?'

'At least I have the difficult conversation, Antonietta. At least I don't run from it.'

'That's unfair.'

'Why? Would you prefer it if I just take off and leave and then write you a letter in a few months, explaining my actions? Would you prefer that I return in five years and expect to resume where we left off?'

'Of course not.'

'So what *do* you want, Antonietta?' he asked. 'You tell me that you are no longer coming to my suite and yet you secretly want me to dissuade you?'

'No!' she protested, but that wasn't quite true. 'Perhaps…' she conceded.

Her honesty floored him and made it hard to remain cold, for he could see the confusion in her eyes.

Cleanly, Rafe.

He didn't want it to be over, though. And neither did she.

'One moment.'

He went into the bedroom and from the dresser there removed a slim black velvet box. Then he returned to the lounge and handed it to her.

Antonietta opened it with some difficulty, for she could feel him watching her. She refused to gasp, but held her breath when she saw the gorgeous pendant, with a stone so bold and blue that for a moment she could imagine she was back in the Blue Grotto.

'Thank you,' she said, 'but I cannot accept it.'

'Of course you can.'

'No.' She held out the box to him but he refused to take it, so she placed it on the desk. 'Rafe, I don't know its value, but I am certain that sapphire would buy me a house—not that I would ever sell it.'

He did not tell her that it was a rare blue diamond. Instead he let her speak.

'But how on earth could I keep it?' She looked at him. 'When my life moves on, am I to wear it for special occasions? Perhaps on my wedding day?'

His jaw ground down.

'No,' she answered her own question. 'For that would be crass. So just on dates, or birthdays, or whatever? Or do I buy a safe? And when my lover asks how I came upon it do I tell him that for a few nights I slept with a prince?'

She looked at him, this girl with the saddest eyes, but still there were no tears.

'I don't think that would go down too well.'

She held it out but still he did not take it from her.

'Please, Rafe, don't mark the end of us with this.'

'Take it, Antonietta. Sell it if you have to.'

'I already told you—I refuse to be your whore.'

She stood and placed the box on an occasional table.

'I'm going.' No more kisses, no promises, just one plea. 'Don't get in touch with me. Don't enquire about me from Aurora or Nico. Don't keep me on a thread.'

And so he did what Antonietta wanted and what his mother had suggested—he pushed them to the point of no return.

'That's very conceited of you, Antonietta. I won't even remember your name by the middle of next week. Certainly I won't be looking you up for a replay. You weren't *that* good.'

Ah, yes, Antonietta thought, *he warned me how cold he would be at the end.*

But she had so little to compare this with—so little to go on apart from her heart, which was braver than she. So she walked over to him and looked up to meet his eyes.

And as it turned out she *could* have the difficult conversation.

'Liar.'

She was met with silence.

'I'm going to get on with my life now.'

She walked out of his suite and there, waiting in the cloister, was Francesca.

'I'm proud of you,' Francesca said.

'So am I,' Antonietta admitted.

And so too was Rafe.

'I hope you have had a wonderful stay,' said the concierge.

'Indeed,' Rafe replied, and handed Pino a handwritten note of thanks, as a royal prince was expected to do to someone who had taken such care to ensure his every demand had been met. 'Thank you for your help. The running route you suggested was most excellent.'

'It was a favourite of mine.'

'Was?' Rafe checked.

'I used to walk there with Rosa.'

Ah, yes, Rafe recalled that Pino had lost his

wife earlier this year. What *was* it with this place? Usually he did not get involved in staff's lives or dramas.

'It's still beautiful,' Rafe said.

'Not without Rosa,' Pino responded, and held out his hand to the Prince. 'It's been a pleasure having you at the Old Monastery, and I know we are all looking forward to your return.'

But he would not be returning.

Like Pino, the thought of being here without his love meant Silibri had lost its charm.

Love?

Instantly he refuted that. His life would still be beautiful without Antonietta, Rafe told himself. He would return to his country and marry a suitable woman, if it pleased the people, and then he would have the power he required for the changes he craved.

He would no longer be the reckless Playboy Prince.

And Antonietta would move on with her life.

She had been expecting that sound.

Chi-Chi was eating a guest's grapes in one of the standard suites as Antonietta switched off the vacuum. She could hear the whirr of the rotors in the distance and headed to the window.

First she saw Pino and one of the bell boys, carrying luggage, and then she saw Rafe, running across the ground and bounding up into the helicopter.

'He's leaving, then,' Chi-Chi said with a distinct lack of interest.

Antonietta didn't have the energy to respond, and she watched as it lifted into the sky until it was just a tiny black dot on the horizon.

Without his 'amusement' Rafe had not even seen out the day…

CHAPTER TWELVE

RAFE'S HELICOPTER TOOK him to Palermo, and from there it was a private jet to Tulano.

Rafael did not reside at the main palace. He had his own court. As the gates opened it was already dark. But there was no question of sleep. He sat with a pen and tried to work on the most important speech of his life.

It took all night, and, when he finally stood before his father, to his disquiet his mother was there, and her cool gaze was less than encouraging.

At least she was listening. His father didn't even let him past the second line.

'She's a commoner?' the King interjected. *'Non.'*

'Will you at least hear what I have to say?' Rafe bit down on his frustration, for he knew it was imperative that he stay polite.

'There's no point,' the King said. 'So I don't

need to hear it. I have been giving your marriage a lot of thought, and we need someone who is well-versed in royal tradition—someone who understands that the crown comes before everything…'

'So a loveless marriage?' Rafe checked.

'Rafe, you have had your freedom, and you have abused that freedom to the nth degree. You are thirty years old and the only heir to the throne—'

'Whose fault is that?' his mother interrupted.

Rafe closed his eyes in frustration. *Here we go*, he thought.

Except his mother truly was the Ice Queen, and Rafe watched as she spoke of the most painful part of her life without a shred of emotion.

'You married me because your father instructed you to. You have stayed married to me purely to avoid a royal scandal, and yet you have created many a royal scandal of your own.'

'And whose fault is *that*?' the King retorted, and he shot a reproving look at the wife who for so long had refused to share his bed.

'Don't speak to her like that,' Rafe warned his father.

'May I remind you to whom you—?'

'I don't need to be reminded,' Rafe retorted. 'I have lived it, and so has your Queen.'

His mother was on his side, Rafe realised. And suddenly he understood her cold nature better and looked back on his childhood with adult eyes. No wonder she had never set foot on Capri, for Rafe could not even fathom taking his future wife there after what he and Antonietta had shared.

He did have his mother's heart after all. She was not cold. She was just bruised by an unfaithful husband, and yet she spoke out for her son now.

'I shall never recommend that you force our son to do the same,' she said.

'I tell you this much,' Rafe said, for though he was grateful to his mother for speaking out he knew his own mind. 'I will never conform to the same.' He faced his father. 'As I have stated, I refuse to take marital advice from you, but I venture to give you some in return: sort out your own marriage before you meddle in mine.'

'How dare you?' the King roared. 'Have you forgotten I am your King?'

'Never,' Rafe responded. 'And for that reason, and that reason only, I stand before you and petition for your permission to propose to the woman I love.'

'She is a commoner,' the King dismissed.

'I have made my choice,' Rafe said.

'A poor one! I will *never* approve this marriage.'

Rafe knew his father well enough to know that he would not back down.

'Will you abide by my decision?' the King demanded.

Would he?

Rafe knew that although his father was King in truth it was Rafe who held the power, for he could simply say no, he would *not* abide by his father's decision. And he would get his own way for his father would loathe the thought of the succession continuing with Rafe's cousins rather than following his own line.

But marrying without the King's permission, even if he remained Crown Prince, would prove a living hell for Antonietta. She would be frozen out by the courtiers and treated with derision by the aides. There would be division in the palace and ramifications that he would not wish on the girl with the saddest eyes, who had only ever wanted to belong.

'Rafe?' the King pushed. 'Will you abide by my decision?'

'Yes,' Rafe said finally. 'I will abide by your decision but I will never forgive you for it.'

'Don't threaten me, Rafe.'

'It is not a threat—it is a fact. And one you should consider. Unlike you, I will do everything in my power to make my marriage work. My wife will never know that I did not wish to marry her. When she asks why I am cold with my father the King I will never tell her the true reason. And when she asks why I don't stand by your side on the balcony I will tell her that it is to do with ancient history and not something she should trouble herself with. And when the heirs you seek are born, and they ask why they only see their grandparents on formal occasions, I will tell them to ask their grandfather to explain why relationships are strained.'

'How dare you threaten me?'

The King stood, but Rafe did not flinch.

'It is a mere glimpse into the future,' Rafe said. 'So think long and hard, Your Majesty, as to how you wish to proceed.'

CHAPTER THIRTEEN

'YOU ARE TENSE,' Antonietta commented as she massaged Vincenzo's shoulders.

As part of her training she was still practising on the staff, but they were actually asking for her now, and a couple of them had told her that they would be her clients if she ever set up on her own.

'Isn't everyone tense at Christmas?' asked Vincenzo, who was lying face-down.

'No!' Antonietta smiled. 'It's supposed to be a happy time.'

'Well, you should be happy!' Vincenzo said. 'It would seem you made the right choice!'

'Sorry?'

'With Sylvester. You know…because his wife left him?'

Her hands stilled on Vincenzo's shoulders.

'You haven't heard?'

'No,' Antonietta said.

As Vincenzo spoke on she discovered that it had been a terrible break-up—and, no, it did not make her happy to hear it.

She poured more oil on her hands and got to work on Vincenzo's knotted neck. Some clients preferred silence, which Antonietta was very good at, and usually Vincenzo was one of them, but today he seemed keen to talk.

'I am so over Christmas, and it isn't even here yet,' Vincenzo said.

'You're off to Florence tonight?' Antonietta checked.

'Yes, but my family are driving me crazy.' He sighed. 'They expect me to come home, yet they don't want me to bring a guest…'

Antonietta's hands paused and, unseen by Vincenzo, she frowned, though she kept her voice light. 'My family don't want me home with or without a guest, so I win.'

He laughed and relaxed a little. 'I don't know how to keep everyone happy,' he admitted.

'I think it's time to make your own traditions, Vincenzo. I know I've been relying on other people to make this Christmas a happy one.'

An idea was forming, though she did not

share it with Vincenzo as he was now half asleep. But when he was done, and it was time for her break, Antonietta knocked on Francesca's door.

'Come in, Antonietta,' Francesca said.

'I lied to you.'

Antonietta saw Francesca's curious frown as she took a seat in her office.

'About what?' Francesca asked. 'Are you intending to open a bordello here?'

They shared a small smile before Antonietta answered. 'Of course not. But I do want to take advantage of my friendship with Aurora and Nico. I wanted to speak with you about it beforehand. I don't want to go over your head.'

'I'm curious,' Francesca admitted.

'I came to Silibri hoping for a wonderful Christmas,' Antonietta said, 'and I've realised I have done little to bring it about.'

Francesca frowned.

'I have left my fate in other people's hands for too long,' Antonietta said. 'I have been waiting for my parents to decide how I spend my days, and what will make me happy, but no more.'

'What do you have in mind?'

'Cake,' Antonietta said. 'And lots of it. And decorations. And a feast shared with the people I care about and who care about me.'

'Who?' Francesca asked.

'You!' Antonietta smiled. 'And anyone else who isn't getting the Christmas they hoped for. Of course it would only take place after all the guests have been taken care of...'

'I have loathed Christmas ever since my divorce,' Francesca admitted—and then perked up. 'We could use the grand dining room,' Francesca said. 'Tony would cook, I'm sure of it, and Pino...' She gave a pained sigh. 'I have been so worried about him spending Christmas alone.'

'And me,' Antonietta admitted.

'I was going to invite him over for dinner,' Francesca admitted, 'but you know how the villagers talk...'

'Believe me, I know,' Antonietta said. 'But of course you are just being...' She was about to say that of course Francesca was just being friendly, but her voice trailed off as her manager went a little bit pink.

Francesca and Pino?

But Pino was grieving Rosa so deeply he would never look at Francesca in that way, Antonietta was sure.

Oh, love was so difficult and cruel—but, given that she couldn't fix her own love-life, she certainly couldn't help anyone else with theirs, so she got back to organising the party.

'We would need Nico's permission.'

'He will never give it.' Francesca shook her head. 'He is like the Grinch. He didn't even want a Christmas tree in the foyer.'

'It's his first Christmas with Aurora and his first as a father…'

'Do you think Aurora could persuade him?'

'Oh, yes.' Antonietta smiled.

'Then on this occasion,' Francesca said, 'I have no problem with you going over my head.'

Antonietta called Aurora. And since Aurora thought it a brilliant idea she said she would be delighted to 'work on Nico'.

'Ha-ha!' Aurora added.

Antonietta would have frowned at that just a few short weeks ago. She had been utterly clueless back then.

'Enjoy!' Antonietta said instead, and then communicated her response back to Francesca.

'We have the go-ahead? Nico approves?' Francesca checked.

'Aurora is working on him.'

'Lucky Aurora!'

Soon they had gathered all the staff who would be working on Christmas Day.

'Do we get paid for staying on?' Chi-Chi asked.

'It's a party,' Francesca said. 'Of course not.'

'Then you can count me out,' Chi-Chi said, and left.

'Well, I think it's a great idea,' Pino said. 'I've been dreading Christmas. I know I said I didn't mind that my daughter is with her husband's family, but really…'

As it turned out, he wasn't the only one who felt lonely at this time of year.

Vera, who worked in the laundry, and could have had the day off but had chosen to work, was another who admitted she struggled. 'I can make a lasagne,' she said.

'No, *I* am making the lasagne,' Tony insisted. 'But, Vera, your cannelloni is the best I have ever tasted…' His voice trailed off as Vincenzo came in.

'What's going on?' Vincenzo asked.

'We're having a meal—a staff party for those who have to…' Antonietta paused '…for those who have *chosen* to work on Christmas Day.'

'Oh!' Vincenzo just stood there.

'Well, it doesn't apply to *you*,' Tony said rather spitefully. '*You're* spending Christmas with family.'

Though it was not quite the perfect remedy for getting over a broken heart, it was fun to organise everything, and in her time off Antonietta baked.

And cried.

But mainly she baked.

Or mainly she cried.

But there was cake involved, which always helped.

What didn't help was finding on Christmas Eve the coffee-flavoured Modica chocolate that she had bought for Rafe.

Well, not really. But she had certainly bought

it with Rafe in mind, never knowing that that very night they would make love.

It had been so good.

At least it had been for her.

But then she reminded herself of his cruel departure, and those horrible harsh words, and told herself to get over him.

And she would.

Oh, she would…

But first she had to weep for him.

Yet she knew that once she'd started she wouldn't be able to stop.

She would have to mourn him later, Antonietta decided. For now, the show must go on.

And so, dressing for the Christmas Eve bonfire that night, she put on the gorgeous dress, tights and boots he had bought her.

And though there was no sign of Rafe's black helicopter, still a chariot awaited…

Well, the hotel put on a car to take the people who were working till late into the village for the last hour of the bonfire before everyone headed to church.

Poor Pino, Antonietta thought as she climbed

in. He looked pensive as they drove up the winding hill.

But then he gave her a little pep talk. 'If there are any problems tonight, just come and find me.'

'I'll be fine, Pino. My family might not be talking to me, but they're not going to make a scene at the Christmas Eve bonfire.'

'You probably haven't heard the news,' said Francesca.

'I know about Sylvester,' Antonietta said.

'It's nothing to do with you, of course,' Francesca soothed, 'but from what I've heard emotions are a little raw.'

'Emotions are always a little raw with the Riccis.' Antonietta shrugged. 'You're right—Sylvester and his marriage are nothing to do with me.'

She shut down the conversation—and not just because she refused to gossip. She shut down the conversation because it hurt. Though she had no feelings at all for Sylvester, another person's misery still didn't feel like a triumph. There was enough sadness in the world, and right now she was busy dealing with her own.

Antonietta was at the start of her life without Rafe. Oh, they had been together for only a short time, but it had been long enough for her heart to know it was love.

The bonfire would be a nice place to weep unnoticed.

It was huge. The children were all laughing and playing, and there were cheers and celebrations as the orange flames licked up towards the sky—she would blame the smoke for her watery eyes, should anyone see. But she refused to break down completely.

'Antonietta...'

She turned at the sound of her name, and there stood her *mamma*.

'Have you heard about Sylvester?'

'What does that have to do with me?'

'It would seem you were right to have doubts,' her mother said. 'Come to us tomorrow,' she offered. 'Have Christmas Day with your family.'

It was everything she had once wished for. Everything she had come to Silibri for.

And yet Rafe had been right when he'd asked her if she would ever be able to forgive her parents. It had seemed a ridiculous question at the time, but it made perfect sense now.

Antonietta looked at her mother, and though she could stand there now, vindicated and redeemed in her mother's eyes, there was too much hurt.

'I have plans for tomorrow,' Antonietta said.

'Antonietta, don't do this. I have missed you so much…'

'Then why didn't you pick up the phone?' Antonietta retorted, and walked off.

'Hey,' Pino said. 'Is everything all right?'

'I got what I wanted,' Antonietta said. 'Or what I thought I wanted. But it's too little, too late.'

'So carry on the fight, then,' Pino said. 'And we can all be miserable this Christmas.'

He made her smile.

'I know that I don't want to be miserable any longer,' Pino said. 'I was talking to Signor Dupont before he left. He told me to go and look at the ruins. Said that life can still be beautiful even without Rosa.'

'He told you that?' Antonietta said. It angered her rather than soothed her, for she loathed the thought of Rafe just going on with his beautiful life.

'He did. And if he hadn't been a guest—and a royal one at that—I might have hit him,' Pino said.

'But you didn't?'

'No, because I think he might be right. I want to make peace with the past, and I want to embrace the rest of my life. Call me old-fashioned, but I believe life is better with family.'

'Even when they hurt you?'

'Of course,' Pino said. 'Love isn't always easy. My daughter has hurt me...'

'Have you told her?'

'No,' Pino said. 'For there might come a time when I hurt her too. I just have to hope she'll be happy for me...'

Was he talking about Francesca? Antonietta pondered. Surely it was too soon? But then, who was she to judge?

She looked at Pino's tired, kind face and gave him a little squeeze on the arm. 'I'd be happy for you, Pino.'

He'd given her good advice. And so she walked over to her mother, who stood by the fire, when it would have been so much easier, even justified, to walk away.

'I have plans tomorrow, Mamma, but I could come over in the evening, perhaps, for a drink.'

And biscotti and cake and *pizzelles*, no doubt. For there was no such thing as *just a drink* in Silibri.

It would be awkward, and difficult, but it would be a start—and, wrongly or rightly, she could not turn her back on her family.

'I'd love that,' said her *mamma*.

'I'll see you tomorrow.'

'You're not coming to church?'

'No.' Antonietta gave a wry smile. 'That would be too many Riccis under the same roof for me.'

Her *mamma* actually smiled.

And Antonietta smiled too, until she got home. And then she gave in to tears and cried more than she ever had.

She was home.

All was sorted.

Except she had let her heart go to a playboy.

And she didn't know how to even start to get it back.

CHAPTER FOURTEEN

'Buon Natale!' Pino said as she came to the door.

'Buon Natale!' Antonietta smiled.

And then she laughed as she stepped into the foyer. Nico had let them pull out all the stops, and there was now a small nativity scene on the reception desk.

'We have bon-bons.' Francesca beamed as she came over. 'And Signor Caruso is throwing in champagne. Aurora must have been working overtime on him.'

And, despite her blue heart, Antonietta laughed. '*Buon Natale*, Francesca.'

She was so grateful for her wonderful friends and colleagues who had supported her. And she was grateful too for Francesca. Yes, her words had hurt at the time, but Antonietta knew she had got off very lightly.

Well, not that lightly, because she still had to

work with Chi-Chi, and they had been given a full list of suites to service in an impossibly short amount of time while the guests were at breakfast or the Oratory or church.

'My back is killing me,' Chi-Chi grumbled.

'One more suite,' Antonietta said, and knocked on the door.

'Good,' Chi-Chi said. 'They're out.'

The suite looked like a tornado had hit it. There were champagne bottles and glasses in the lounge, half-drunk mimosas on the bedside tables, and wrapping paper all over the bed.

'Don't just throw it away,' Antonietta barked, as Chi-Chi scooped up the paper. 'There might still be gifts in there…'

Foolish words.

'My back is killing me,' Chi-Chi grumbled. She sat on the sofa and commenced her *slowly-slowly*, folding the wrapping paper piece by piece as Antonietta made the bed. 'I just need five minutes.'

Antonietta rolled her eyes as Chi-Chi turned the television on. Really! She wanted a few moments alone and so, having made the bed, she went and serviced the bathroom. For a tiny second she allowed herself the dream of her and Rafe sitting in bed on Christmas morning, sipping mimosas as they unwrapped their presents.

Did she regret her time with Rafe?

No, not for a single second.

Oh, she regretted that they had been doomed from the start…and perhaps she regretted how hard she had tumbled into loving him.

But no, she refuted, she did not regret that.

As she came out of the bathroom she glanced at the television and saw the Vatican, and the Pope giving his Christmas address.

Antonietta stood watching for a moment, and saw an image of the Christmas celebrations in France, and then Germany, and then the British royal family heading to church…

And then her difficult Christmas became an impossible one—for there were the King and Queen of Tulano on the palace balcony, and beside them stood Crown Prince Rafael.

It was a mere glimpse, but it burned in her brain: the sight of Rafe in all his military splendour, looking so impossibly handsome and so utterly beyond her, and worst of all so happy, for he had been smiling. Smiling a natural, relaxed smile that told Antonietta he was truly happy.

Of course she wanted him to be happy—but not quite yet. Not when her own heart was so raw and bleeding.

But even as Antonietta cried out in recognition the footage moved on to Austria, and how Christmas was being celebrated there.

'He's mean,' Chi-Chi huffed. 'Do you know, he left letters for all the staff who had dealings with him, and a tip, yet he left nothing for me?'

'Nor me,' Antonietta said.

Well, he had tried to give her a necklace. But that was one thing that didn't make sense.

It could not be a coincidence that the sapphire he'd tried to give her had been the exact shade of the water in the Blue Grotto. Surely?

Get over yourself, Antonietta, she warned herself.

He probably had a collection of sapphires. And all the women he took to the Blue Grotto and made love to were probably gifted one.

There was probably a Blue Grotto Sapphire club, Antonietta decided bitterly.

'Time for me to go,' Chi-Chi declared at five minutes to three. '*Buon Natale*, Antonietta.'

'*Buon Natale*, Chi-Chi.'

But *was* it a happy Christmas?

Antonietta brushed her hair and applied Aurora's red lipstick, which clashed a little with her Persian orange dress.

She had managed to get a replacement lipstick for her friend, and had baked gifts for everyone else. Well, everyone except Pino.

Antonietta collected her gifts from her locker and arrived only a little late to the party she had herself organised. And suddenly it really was a *Buon Natale*.

There was a canopy of lights that stretched across the ballroom, and in the corner stood a huge tree dressed in ropes of lights. It reminded her so much of her magical time in Capri that for a moment tears filled her eyes.

'Who did this?' she asked.

Francesca didn't even have to answer her, for a moment later there were footsteps, and Antonietta turned to the sight of Nico carrying little Gabe, with Aurora by his side.

'You're here!' Antonietta beamed. 'And you've

been so busy!' she exclaimed. 'The ballroom looks beautiful.'

'Doesn't it?' Aurora said as she hugged her. 'And of course I'm here. To tell the truth, my family were driving me crazy. It is wonderful to escape!'

'There is no escape…' Nico sighed. 'And we have to head back by five for an announcement.'

'Announcement?' Antonietta frowned.

'Don't pretend you don't know,' Aurora said, and then blinked. 'My brother is getting engaged.'

'Oh!'

'To Chi-Chi!' Aurora groaned.

'No!'

'Yes,' Nico groaned. 'How the hell do I fire her now! Antonietta, you cannot leave Silibri. I swear the two of them will move into the cottage and we'll never get them out.'

For the first time since Rafe had left, Antonietta found that she was properly laughing. 'Every pot has its lid!' she said.

'And that lid is going to be my sister-in-law!' Aurora sighed, but then brightened when she saw Vincenzo arriving, weighed down with presents. 'I thought you were off!'

'I am,' Vincenzo said. 'But since when did I ever miss a party?'

Antonietta frowned, a little surprised that Vincenzo wasn't in Florence. But then Tony walked in, carrying silver trays laden with seafood and all kinds of delicacies, smiling proudly. He almost overbalanced when he saw that Vincenzo had arrived.

She turned and looked as a flush crept up Vincenzo's cheeks when Tony smiled at him. *Oh, my!* No wonder Vincenzo was putting on weight. Imagine if Tony was trying to constantly feed you!

'Is Tony the reason you aren't home for Christmas?' Antonietta asked with a smile.

'I *am* home for Christmas,' Vincenzo said. 'Here is home. It just took me a little while to work that out. My family have refused to accept Tony and me. So it is time to start our own traditions…'

'Good for you,' Antonietta said.

The table was groaning with the most delicious food. Christmas Eve was the Feast of the

Seven Fishes, and there was lobster, *scungilli*… And as they sat and laughed it was impossible not be happy.

As the feasting ended the speeches started, and she looked around the table and saw that these people were the ones she loved.

Nico started by thanking his staff, and Antonietta for her marvellous idea. And there was clearly too much champagne flowing, because they all toasted Aurora for persuading him.

Then Francesca spoke. 'My staff have never let me down…'

Antonietta flushed a little at that.

'Never,' Francesca said. 'There is nowhere I would rather be than here this Christmas.'

And then Antonietta stood, and though her speech was short and sweet it came from her heart. 'I am so lucky to have you all.'

She truly was, Aurora knew. She finally had her magical Christmas.

'I might go for a walk in the temple ruins,' said Pino. 'And burn this dinner off.'

'A good idea!' Francesca smiled.

For a second Antonietta thought Francesca

was going to suggest joining Pino, but there was something in his stance that suggested he wanted to be alone.

'Enjoy your walk,' Francesca said.

'Thank you.' Pino smiled.

But one day Francesca would join him. Antonietta just knew it.

It really was a two-by-two world, Antonietta thought as she bounced little Gabe on her knee and looked over to Vincenzo and Tony, who were happily holding hands.

'Antonietta,' Francesca whispered in her ear. 'Sorry to pull you away, but I need someone to take a trolley up to the August Suite.'

And it seemed that 'someone' would be her.

'Here,' Antonietta said, and handed little Gabe back to Aurora. 'I have to take a trolley up. I shouldn't be long.'

'We ought to get going,' Aurora said.

'Yes.' Antonietta forced a smile. 'You have an announcement to get to.'

Antonietta could hear the laughter wafting up from the ballroom as she pushed the trolley along the cloister. She hadn't been back to the

August Suite since her cruel parting from Rafe, and it didn't help that it was Christmas Day.

And that everyone was happy except her.

She pressed her fingers into her eyes and rued the champagne she had drunk, because guests did not need a chambermaid with tears in her eyes.

'Service,' she called after knocking.

When she got no reply, she swiped her card and let herself in.

'Service,' she said again.

And then stepped into a room that was not in complete darkness, for though the drapes were drawn, every candle in the suite had been lit. The August Suite was softly illuminated with twinkling lights that stretched and danced to a gentle breeze she hadn't even been aware existed.

It felt like a church, or a ballroom, as if the stars had been brought down from the sky.

'*Buon Natale*, Antonietta.'

She jolted at the sound of his voice.

'Rafe!'

She must be dreaming. Hallucinating, even. For he was dressed in military finery, and now that her eyes were adjusting she saw that the August Suite had a Christmas tree, with presents beneath it. And a dining table set for two.

Yes, she was dreaming, Antonietta decided. She would wake up in a moment and her pillow would be wet with tears and she would be late for duty…

'I forgot my present,' Rafe said when she could not speak.

'I gave you your present, Rafe. The neroli oil, remember?'

'Of course. It is on my dresser at home. I meant the chocolate.'

'I gave it to Pino,' Antonietta said, utterly unsure as to what was going on, and expecting him at any moment to disappear.

Except he did not disappear. In fact, when she walked over he wrapped her in his arms, but that only served to confuse her further.

'I saw you on the balcony…on the television,' she said.

'That was a couple of hours ago. It would be a break with tradition if I did not appear…'

'Rafe.' She pulled back. 'I cannot do this. Does Francesca—?'

'Stop,' he said. 'There is no conflict—this is no clandestine meeting. She knows that I am here, and so do Nico and Aurora.'

'They know?'

'Of course. And they agree that Christmas Day should be spent with the people you love. *Oui?*'

Yes. Did that mean birthdays too? And all the other special days? Would he return to Silibri on a whim?

'I have *ravioli caprese* for us,' said Rafe, 'and chocolate torte too…'

'I've eaten, Rafe.'

Perhaps it was not the kindest reply, when he had gone to so much trouble, but Antonietta didn't know what his being here meant.

When she didn't lift the cloche, Rafe did.

But it was not a romantic dinner for two that lay beneath.

It was her Blue Grotto stone. She would recognise it anywhere, even set in a ring.

'It's beautiful, but…'

Rather than pick it up, she cast anxious eyes up to him.

'Please don't play with my heart, Rafe. Please

don't tell me that this sapphire means you will one day return…that we will kiss and be together again in the light of the Blue Grotto…'

'I would never do that,' Rafe said. 'And it is not a sapphire, Antonietta. It is a diamond. Forgive me for ever thinking it should be a pendant. We *shall* kiss and be together again in the light of the Blue Grotto—but as husband and wife…'

'How…?'

'How not?' Rafe said. 'How could I ever marry anyone else? It would not just be unfair to us both, but it would be cruel to my wife also. I have my mother to thank for that insight.'

He told her the truth.

'My father used to take his lovers to Capri, and I confess, for a while I considered doing the same with you. And Nico said that Silibri could be my bolthole…'

'Never!' Antonietta shook her head.

'Silibri can be *our* bolthole,' Rafe said. 'I know it will be a huge change for you, and I know you might need time to think, and it's a lot to take in…'

'No,' Antonietta said. 'I don't need to think—you are my lid.'

'Scusi?'

'Every pot has its lid. And you, Rafe, are mine.' She picked up her Blue Grotto ring and placed it on her own finger. 'I would love more than anything in the world to be your wife.'

And then, when her bravery ran out, when she was daunted by all that lay ahead, Rafe carried her to the candlelit bedroom where he made her his lover for life.

EPILOGUE

'I HAVE TO go to my parents' house later…'

They lay in bed as she stared at her ring, which sparkled in the fading candlelight.

'I said I would go there for a drink.'

'You are speaking to each other now?' Rafe checked.

'It would seem so.'

'That is good,' Rafe said. 'Tell them that I have married you.'

'Not yet!' Antonietta laughed. 'You must ask my father's permission!'

'Oh, no,' Rafe said. 'We will be married by then.'

'Don't be ridiculous.'

'There will be a huge formal wedding in a few weeks,' Rafe told her. 'And there will be duty and cameras and parades…' He looked over at his bride-to-be. 'But I want you to know how committed I am before I take you home. Life is going to change for you, Antonietta…'

'I know.'

'But my love for you never will.'

'I know that too,' Antonietta said. 'But, Rafe, I have nothing—and I mean *nothing*—to wear.'

Enter Aurora. The best friend, the best seamstress and the best keeper and sharer of secrets that a girl could ever have.

Antonietta's dress was a sheath of Italian white lace, so slender that for a second Antonietta was sure that Aurora had got her measurements wrong.

'Hold still,' Aurora warned. She wore gloves just to do the zipper up. 'Oh, Antonietta, look!'

Aurora was crying—she actually was—as she admired not only her handiwork, and the pretty shoes she had selected, but her best friend's happiness.

And then Francesca arrived and dotted her hair with flowers, handed her a little posy.

'I am so happy for you,' Francesca said. 'And I take back every word I said about him.'

It was the most intimate and unofficial wedding in Tulano history. But what it lacked in paperwork, it made up for with love.

Rafe slid a heavy ring on her finger and said, 'I loved you the morning I met you, though I told myself I had a head injury.' Everyone smiled. 'And I hope every day to see your eyes smiling.'

And Antonietta smiled up at her impossibly handsome groom and said, 'I love you, and that is never going to change.'

'I know,' Rafe told her, and he kissed his shy bride who melted solely for him.

He held her hand as Pino read her favourite verse from Corinthians and choked up a little, for it was the one that had been read at his and Rosa's wedding. One that was still relevant now…

'"And now these three remain: faith, hope and love. But the greatest of these is love."'

And Nico did a speech, during which both Aurora and Antonietta sat, just a little tense, hoping he would not share too much of the groom's chequered past.

He did not.

'Aurora considers Antonietta family. So I

guess,' Nico said, looking over to Rafe, 'that my old friend is now almost my brother-in-law. Welcome to our family.'

Christmas had delivered its magic.

With Rafe by her side she belonged in this world.

And with friends like these surrounding her as she danced with the love of her life, Antonietta had got her for ever family…

* * * * *